Dragonlore

From the Archives of
the Grey School of Wizardry

Dragonlore

From the Archives of
the Grey School of Wizardry

By Ash "LeopardDancer" DeKirk

New Page Books
A Division of The Career Press, Inc.
Franklin Lakes, NJ

OBERON ZELL PRESENTS DRAGONLORE
EDITED AND TYPESET BY GINA TALUCCI
INTERIOR ILLUSTRATIONS BY IAN DANIELS AND ERIF THUNAN
Cover design by Lu Rossman/Digi Dog Design NYC
Interior Illustrations by Ian Daniels and Erif Thunan
Printed in the U.S.A. by Book-mart Press

To order this title, please call toll-free 1-800-CAREER-1 (NJ and Canada: 201-848-0310) to order using VISA or MasterCard, or for further information on books from Career Press.

The Career Press, Inc., 3 Tice Road, PO Box 687,
Franklin Lakes, NJ 07417
www.careerpress.com
www.newpagebooks.com

Library of Congress Cataloging-in-Publication Data

DeKirk, Ash, 1978-
    Oberon Zell presents dragonlore : from the archives of the Grey School of Wizardry / by Ash "LeopardDancer" DeKirk.
        p. cm.
    Includes bibliographical references and index.
    ISBN-13: 978-1-56414-868-1
    ISBN-10: 1-56414-868-8
        1. Dragons. I. Title. II. Title: Dragonlore

GR830.D7D45 2006
398′.469--dc22

2006012459

Dedication

This book is dedicated to Mrs. D.R. McFarquar,
a true inspiration to all.

—Ash "LeopardDancer" DeKirk

To Jasmine and John with love.

—Ian Daniels

I wish to thank Ash for the opportunity to work with her
and achieve a mutual vision. Also, I give heartfelt thanks to Morgan
and Rainbird for their advice and support, to Oberon for his graceful
mediation, to my partner Bill for his loving patience, and to all the Little
Folk who asked me for dragons.

—Erif Thunen

Acknowledgments

First and foremost, I would like to thank Oberon Zell-Ravenheart,
without whom this book never would have come about.
And to my friends and family who put up with me during this process
and gave me support and help when it was most needed.

Contents

Chapter 2: Dragon Myths of the World   63

Foreword

"Here There Be Dragons!"

By Oberon Zell-Ravenheart

Dragons! Who has not been fascinated and intrigued by these mighty and mysterious reptiles of myth and legend? It seems they have always been with us, stalking and raging through our stories, our dreams, and our fantasies. Our oldest epic saga, the tale of Gilgamesh, King of Uruk in Sumeria (modern Iraq) dates to 2700 B.C.E. In it, the King of Uruk and his wild man companion, Enkidu, battle Humbaba, the dragon who guards the forest of the Cedars of Lebanon.

Story after story of dragon encounters echo down the annals of history. The Babylonian God Marduk slew Tiamet—the great female dragon of the bitter sea, and out of her body created the foundations of the Earth. The Greek God Zeus overcame Typhon, the cosmic Dragon of Gaea, in the Battle of the Titans. Apollo killed the Delphic Python to claim the world's most famous oracular site as his own. The Greek hero Perseus rescued

Princess Andromeda from the sea monster Cetus by displaying the severed head of the Gorgon Medusa, thus turning the beast to stone.

The mighty Heracles slew the many-headed Lernean Hydra as his second labor. Jason, leader of the Argonauts, defeated the armed warriors who sprang from dragon's teeth sown in a field he plowed with fire-breathing oxen, and then killed the dragon that guarded the Golden Fleece. Odysseus lost three sailors to the horrible Hydra Scylla. The Hebrew hero Daniel killed the dragon of Babylon, which got him thrown into the lion's den as punishment. An image of this dragon was inlaid in the magnificent Ishtar Gate of Babylon, now known as the Sirrush.

The young Wizard Merlyn Ambrosius won praise with his prophetic vision of battling dragons—one red and one white—beneath the unstable tower of Vortigern. The German hero Siegfried impaled the ferocious Fafnir, and gained knowledge of the speech of birds from a few drops of its blood. The famous English knight Saint George slew his dragon, symbolizing the defeat of Satan by Christ. Saint Martha subdued the Tarasque of France, tied her belt around its neck, and led it docilely into the town of Nerlue, where the villagers killed it with stones and spears, and renamed the town Tarascon. The town commemorates this event in annual processions to this very day. And the famous little hobbit Bilbo Baggins faced and outwitted the terrible fire-breathing dragon Smaug on the Lonely Mountain.

For centuries, maps drawn by explorers and seafarers designated the blank lands beyond the boundaries of the known world with the familiar warning: "Here there be dragons." Sightings of giant sea serpents have been solemnly attested to by generations of mariners. Cryptozoological investigators continue to probe the murky depths of Loch Ness, Lake Champlain, Loch Morag, Lake Ogopogo, and many other lakes whose abyssal waters are believed by many to harbor living prehistoric monsters, such as Nessie, Champ, Moraga, and Pogo. Other explorers have mounted expeditions to the swampy jungles of Africa's Congo Basin in search of the legendary Mokele-Mbembe, which is described by locals as a long-necked sauropod.

After all these thousands of years, dragons still thrill and fascinate us. They roar and soar out of the pages of sci-fi and fantasy books like *DragonLance, Flight of Dragons, Dragonology,* and Anne McCaffrey's wonderful *Dragon Riders of Pern* trilogy. They dominate the silver screens in movies such as *Dragonslayer, Dragonheart, Dragonworld, The Neverending Story, Reign of Terror,* and *Lord of the Rings: Return of the King.* They are even featured in major TV documentaries, such as Animal Planet's amazing 2005 special, *Dragon's World: A Fantasy Made Real.* And an entire lucrative genre of immensely popular role-playing and video games has been spawned by the original *Dungeons & Dragons* game.

I'll never forget my first encounter with dragons. Of course, I'd come across mentions of dragons in the books of myths and fairy tales that comprised my earliest childhood reading, I had not seriously considered them any more than the many other fabulous creatures, gods, heroes, fairies, and monsters I encountered within those pages. All were delightful, of course, but they were also clearly imaginary fabrications of fantasy, not "real" in any concrete sense.

And then I began public school and encountered libraries! Suddenly my literary vistas expanded to limitless horizons as I discovered worlds upon worlds of books beyond my modest collection at home. I practically moved into the school library during lunch and recess, and the town's public library across the street became my favorite after school hangout, as I was determined to explore every topic I found of interest.

I attended elementary school from the late 1940s to the mid-1950s. In those days, every classroom had an identical feature: one side of the room was all windows, beneath which ran a long bookcase the full length of the wall. And in this bookcase were several sets of the *World Book Encyclopedia* to be used for class research assignments. I got it into my head that the best way to acquire a general knowledge would be to read the entire 24 volumes, from beginning to end. So I secured a desk along the window side of each room I was in. In the first weeks of class, I would read all of my textbooks for the semester, just so I'd know the material. And then, one at a time, I would slip out a volume of the *World Book* and hide it behind my class book as I pored over the pages of knowledge.

Volume A, assimilated. Volumes B and C, likewise. Then I began Volume D. And one momentous day I turned the page, and there, under "Dinosaurs," was a two-page spread of Charles Knight's famous painting of a Triceratops facing off against a Tyrannosaurus Rex. And with an indescribable thrill of realization, I suddenly knew: Dragons were real! Just as the stories said, once upon a time, the world was ruled by huge and mighty reptiles. They lumbered over the land, they churned the seas, and they commandeered the air. They were even more immense and diverse than the most outrageous stories had portrayed them...and they really existed!

Well, I became a total "dino kid." I learned everything I could about the amazing creatures. I memorized every dino name I could find and all their statistics: what their Greek names meant, when and where they lived, what they ate, how big they were, and so on. My parents thought this was all rather amazing, as they couldn't even pronounce most of these names, and they'd ask me to come out at their parties and rattle off dino stats for their guests.

I began visiting natural history museums, hunting for fossils, and collecting dino memorabilia—books at first, then models when they started being made, which I would carefully paint in realistic colors. I used to dream of which dino model would come out next! Today I have perhaps one of the most extensive collections of miniature dinosaur replicas in existence, going back more than 50 years. And an entire section of my library is dedicated to dinosaurs—and dragons.

Enter any gift shop today—particularly ones specializing in magickal, mystical, and metaphysical curiosities. There be dragons! You will find dragon figurines, dragon jewelry, dragon calendars, dragon greeting cards, dragon posters, dragon books, dragon T-shirts, even posable dragon action figures! There is even a whole catalog of dragon products called Dancing Dragon Designs.

And now there is this wonderful book, *Dragonlore*. It is the first in a new series of Grey School textbooks, compiled from a course of classes that Ash "LeopardDancer" DeKirk created to teach at the online Grey School of Wizardry, of which I am Headmaster. While this book will be required reading for all students taking her course, the material gathered herein is so fascinating that we felt we just had to share it with all the other dragon aficionados out there. Which, I suspect, includes just about everybody! At least, it includes you and me—right? If you would like to find out more about the Grey School of Wizardry, log-on to *www.GreySchool.com*.

Soar High,
Oberon Zell-Ravenheart
Headmaster
Grey School of Wizardry

Chapter

I

Dragons of
the World

Timeless

*The shadows of creatures
dark against the night.
They are silent, moving
swiftly through the skies.*

*Hulking forms of dragons
flying
through the twilight.
Ageless beasts,
they call out,
the song of times long gone and times to come
full on their breath.*

Many have sought
these guardians of time.
In their memories is
all knowledge of past and present.

Ageless are these creatures
and long are their memories.
They alone hold the key
to all that was and all that will be.
Their voices fill the air,
timeless reminders.

What is a dragon? In modern times the concept of the dragon has become extremely stereotyped. What is the first thing that pops into your mind when you hear the word dragon? Most likely it will be the winged, fire-breathing terror of European myth. But that is not all a dragon can be.

When looking at creatures that could possibly be considered dragons, what does the culture that the creature comes from say about it? Does the culture consider it a dragon? In many cases, snakes and dragons are intertwined in the mythos of a culture. Dragons such as **wurms** can be reminiscent of giant snakes. Some, such as **pythons**, are giant snakes. In other cases dragons and lizards are intertwined. **Drakes** are dragons that lack wings and look just like giant lizards.

So how do we tell what is a dragon and what is not? Below is a list of traits and attributes that the myths and legends of the world grant dragons. If your creature in question has one or more of them, then chances are you would be safe calling it a dragon.

- ❀ reptilian in looks or behavior
- ❀ avian traits such as feathers
- ❀ utilization of fire or poison as a natural defense
- ❀ being associated with water
- ❀ having control over natural occurrences such as the weather, earthquakes, tsunamis, and so forth
- ❀ being the guardian of something, be it treasure or knowledge
- ❀ magickal or supernatural abilities
- ❀ being able to fly, with or without wings
- ❀ shapeshifting ability
- ❀ being viewed as a god or a servant of the gods

Dragons in Asia

Among the Chinese and the Japanese cultures, dragons are a most potent symbol of the beneficent, rain-giving powers of the gods. They are symbols of power, royalty, and sovereignty. Among the Chinese, the dragon is one of the four great protective beasts of the country, along with unicorn, the tortoise, and the phoenix.

Asiatic dragons in general have snake-like bodies, horse-like heads, and four paws with three to four great curving claws apiece. Descriptions by the scholar Wang Fu, during the Han dynasty (206 B.C.–A.D. 220) grant them the horns of a stag, the head of a camel, the eyes of a demon, the neck of a snake, the belly of a clam, the scales of a carp, the talons of an eagle, the feet of a tiger, and the ears of an ox. Asiatic dragons were said to have a total of 117 scales. Of these scales, 81 of them are believed to be imbued with yang energy—the active, dominant, masculine force. The remaining 36 scales are imbued with yin energy—the passive, accepting, feminine force.

Many Asiatic dragons have the ability to change shape as well, turning to human form or a more mundane animal form such as a bird or a fish. Dragons turned human or animal are always exquisite specimens of the species. Humans and other animals may also turn into dragons through various means. In a myth we will look at later, a young boy swallows a dragon pearl, and so becomes a dragon himself. Mages and sages may spend a lifetime seeking the means to turn into one of these great and wise creatures. The Dragon's Gate, located on the Yellow River in China, is a place where fish may be changed into dragons.

There are differences between the male and female Asiatic dragons. Males tend to have more rigid and unruly manes, horns that are thinner near the head and thicker near the outer parts, and are often depicted with clubs in their tails. Females, on the other hand, tend to have nicer, balanced manes, horns thicker at the base and more tapered at the top, and are depicted with fans held in their tails.

The dragon's voices are said to sound like the sweet jingling of bells. Depending on the age and type of dragon, the Asiatic dragons may or may not have wings. Some dragons lack them completely and some do not gain wings until they are fully mature. These dragons can, nevertheless, fly by floating in the air using magic. Dragons may have what the Chinese call a **chi'ih-muh**, a natural looking bump on their foreheads that facilitates wingless flight. Dragons that do not have the chi'ih-muh carry a wand called a **po-shan** that serves the same function. A good example of an Asiatic style dragon lacking wings is Falkor, the Luckdragon of *The Neverending Story*. Falkor also has the bell-like voice of the Asian dragons. Many Asiatic dragons get part of their power from a pearl called a "pearl of wisdom" or "dragon jewel" that they keep tucked under their chins, under their tongues, or embedded in their foreheads.

Chinese Dragons

Dragons have always played an important part in Chinese culture. China's Emperor sat on the Dragon Throne and wore Dragon Robes.

Imperial Dragon

The dragons that adorned the Emperor's robes sported five toes instead of the usual four. These dragons were called **shen-lung** or **Imperial Dragons**. According to myth the first Emperor was the dragon-god Yu. The ordinary people of China even refer to themselves as the Children of the Dragon or the People of the Dragon.

The Chinese Dragon Dance, used today for luck and prosperity and performed during the Chinese New Year, originated as a ritual to encourage rainfall, as dragons were the masters of the rains and waters. Another important Chinese holiday to feature dragons is the Chinese Dragon Boat Festival, during which dragon-shaped boats are raced on all of the country's waterways. This festival is a nation-wide prayer for a good harvest to result from the rains sent by the dragons. Even today, full-fledged belief in dragons exists in China. A good example of this is evident in Repulse Bay, Hong Kong, where an apartment complex built near a mountain was created with a hole in the center to allow the dragon who was said to dwell on the mountain an unobstructed view of the ocean. This was done in the hopes of keeping the dragon's goodwill.

Chinese dragons (and most other Asiatic dragons) live for millenia and undergo many changes throughout their lifetimes. A Chinese dragon is not considered fully mature until it reaches the age of 3,000 years. A baby dragon is hatched from a brilliant, gem-like egg that was laid some 1,000 years before. The newly hatched dragon resembles nothing so much as a very large water snake or eel. When it attains the age of 500 years, the hatchling dragon will gain a head similar to a carp. During this stage, the youngling dragon is known as a **Kiao**. At the age of 1,500 years, the young dragon will have grown four stubby legs with four claws on each paw, an elongated head and tail, and a profuse beard. Now it is called **Kiao-lung**. By the time two millenia have passed, the dragon will have gained horns and a new name, **Kioh-lung**. During the final millenium, it will grow wings. At the age of 3,000 years, the fully grown dragon is named **Ying-lung**. When most people today think of Chinese (or Japanese) dragons, these last two forms are the ones that readily come to mind.

Types of Dragons

Ch'i-lung: These dragons are stuck at the Kiao-lung stage. They lack horns and are tri-colored, being red, white, and green.

Dragon Horse: Dragon horses look like horses but have a dragonesque head and scales instead of fur. Some dragon horses can fly, though none have wings. Most, however, are water dwellers. These creatures are considered divine messengers.

A dragon horse is said to have emerged from the Yellow River and gave the Emperor a circular diagram representing the Yin-Yang. A dragon horse is also said to have emerged from the River Lao and revealed the eight tri-grams of the I-Ching. In the anime series *Inuyasha*, the wolf demon Sesshoumaru travels in a chariot pulled by a two-headed dragon horse.

Chinese Dragon

The Dragon Kings: The five immortal Dragon Kings dwell under the sea in elaborate crystal palaces. One Dragon King is the overall chief, and each of the other four represent one of the Four Cardinal Directions: North, South, East, and West. Their names are Ao Ch'in, Ao Jun, Ao Kuang, and Ao Shun respectively. The Dragon Kings answer to the Jade Emperor, who tells them where to distribute the rains. According to legend, the Dragon Kings are 3–5 miles long with shaggy legs and tails and whiskered muzzles. Their slinky, serpentine bodies are covered in golden scales. It is said that when the Dragon Kings rise to the surface, waterspouts and typhoons are created, and when they take to the air, massive typhoons result. Only the exceptional were chosen to meet with the great ocean sovereigns. The Dragon Kings play a major role in the 16th century Chinese folk legend *Journey to the West* by Wu Cheng'en, in which the Great Sage Equalling Heaven (also called Son Goku or the Monkey King) terrorized the Dragon Kings before being captured and trapped underneath the Mountain of Five Elements. The Dragon Kings show up later in the story to assist Goku in his trials attempting to protect the T'ang Priest Sanzang. In addition to the four oceanic Dragon Kings, there were a few others. Lung Wang is the fifth Dragon King and the master of Fire. Pai Lung is yet another of the Dragon Kings. He is very unique, because he is all white.

Fe-lian and Shen-yi: These are rival dragons. Fe-lian is a Wind god, and he carries a bag of Wind. He is a grand troublemaker and is watched over by Shen-yi, the Great Archer. Fe-lian and Shen-yi serve as balances to one another.

Fu-T'sang Lung: The Fu-T'sang Lung are subterranean dragons. They are guardians of great wealth and great wisdom. The Fu-T'sang Lung are also called treasure dragons, and the best modern example of them is found in the emblem for the popular *Mortal Kombat* game and movie series.

Golden Dragon Yu: Yu is a great golden dragon with a wonderous mane and five claws on each paw. According to the myth, Yu is the dragon that became the first Chinese Emperor, and he is the symbol of the Emperor of China. He is also seen as a symbol of rebirth.

Gou Mang and Rou Shou: These are two of China's cosmic dragons who serve as messengers to the gods. They are ti'en-lung dragons. Gou mang is said to bring good fortune and is a herald for the coming of spring. Rou shou brings bad fortune and heralds the coming of fall.

Great Chi'en-Tang: The master of all River Dragons, he has flaming red scales and a fiery mane. Chi'en-Tang is 900 feet long.

K'uh-lung: These dragons are not born from jeweled eggs. Rather, they are created from seaweed. The K'uh-lung, similar to many other types, are stuck at the Kiao-lung stage of the draconic life cycle. They have webbed feet that are more flipper-like than foot-like. They are entirely aquatic and do not fly.

Lei Chen-tzu: This dragon is a great, green dragon with wings. He also has a boar-like head complete with tushes. Lei Chen-tzu did not begin life as a dragon. He was the son of Lei, the Thunder Dragon, born from a clap of thunder. He was born as a human, but upon eating two magickal apricots, transformed into a dragon. Lei Chen-tzu is often used as a symbol of righteousness and heroism.

Li-lung: The Li-lung are the benevolent dragons of earth, wind, and water. These dragons are said to ascend into the heavens in the forms of typhoons or waterspouts.

Imperial Dragon

Lung: The Lung or "Horned Dragons" are the most powerful of the Chinese dragons even though they are completely deaf. They have the power to call the rains and control the clouds. In art the Lung is depicted with its head pointing to the south and its tail to the north. These dragons are associated with the east and with the sun.

Lung-wang: The lung-wang is a chimeric dragon creature with the body of a human and the head of a dragon. It is associated with the Element of Fire.

Pai Lung: This dragon is another of the Dragon Kings. He is quite unusual in that he is a white dragon. Pai Lung was born of a human mother through a virgin birth. He has dazzling white scales and is a fully matured dragon.

P'an-lung: The P'an-lung are stuck at the Kiao-lung stage of draconic development. They, unlike other types of dragons, can not fly. They do not have wings, a chi'ih-muh, or a po-shan.

Pa Snakes: The Pa are huge, serpentine dragons lacking any limbs or wings at all. The favorite food of the Pa are elephants, so they are most likely found in areas where elephants dwell. When they eat an elephant, they do not spit out the bones for three years!

P'eng-niao: These bird-dragons are rare in Chinese myth. They have the head of a dragon and the wings and lower body of a bird. In some cases, they may have a completely serpentine body with feathered scales, bird-like wings, and bird-like legs and feet.

Pa Snake

Pi-hsi: This chimeric dragon is Lord of the Rivers. Pi-hsi has the shell of an armored tortoise and the feet, tail, and head of a dragon. A modern representation of this dragon shows up in the *Final Fantasy* game series as the giant Adamantoise enemies.

Shin-lung: These are the azure-scaled dragons that bring the winds and rains for the benefit of mankind.

T'ao T'ieh: This is one of the oldest known Chinese dragons. The T'ao T'ieh has one head but two bodies, each with its own tail and set of hind-limbs. This six-legged dragon reperesents gluttony and is used on dishes as a subtle deterrent

Pi-hsi Dragon

to being greedy at the dinner table. T'ao T'ieh is one of the creatures featured in the PlayStation 2 game *Culdcept.*

Yu-lung

Ti'en-lung: The Ti'en-lung are the guardians of the celestial palaces of the gods.

Ying-Long: These dragons are rather unique. They have fur instead of scales and usually have feathered wings. Nall and Ruby from the Playstation games *Lunar: Silver Star Story Complete* and *Lunar 2: Eternal Blue* are good examples of Ying-long dragons.

Yu-lung: The Yu-lung has a fish body and a dragon-like head. Yu-lung are considered very lucky and are often used to represent success in passing exams.

Japanese Dragons

For the most part, Japanese dragons resemble Chinese dragons in appearance and growth. Japanese dragons tend to be more serpentine, however, and they have only three claws as opposed to the four or five on the Chinese dragons. Japanese dragons are the natural enemies of the kitsune, or fox spirits.

Types of Dragons

Fuku-ryu: These are dragons of luck. They end life in the kiao-lung phase, but can fly nonetheless, using the means listed previously for the Chinese dragons. Falkor of *The Neverending Story* is a fuku-ryu.

Han-ryu

Han-ryu: The han-ryu is a multi-colored dragon that is a cousin of the Chinese Ch'i-lung. It is over 40 feet in length. This dragon, so go the legends, will never reach heaven no matter how hard it tries.

Tatsu: These dragons are said to be descended from a primitive variety of three-toed Chinese dragon. The tatsu are more closely linked with the sea than with the rains, as Japan is less likely to suffer from devastating droughts.

Ka-ryu: The Ka-ryu is among the smallest of the Japanese dragons. They have fiery red scales and end their growth in the kiao-lung phase.

Kiyo: This is a dragon that was once a human. It is a symbol of power and vengeance.

Tobi-tatsu: This dragon is serpentine, having a dragon head and the feathered wings and lower body of a bird. Sound familiar? The tobi-tatsu are related to the p'eng-niao of China. These dragons are similar to the amphiteres of Europe and the plumed serpents of the Americas. Another name for these dragons is hai-ryu.

Ri-ryu: These dragons can attain full maturity culminating in the growth of wings. Beyond that, they do have one feature that makes them different from other dragons we have gone over; the ri-ryu have exceptional sight. They can see much farther and with even greater clarity than other dragons.

Ryo-Wo: This is another Japanese Dragon King. It is in charge of the Tidal Jewels, which control the tides of the world. Ryo-wo is credited with giving jellyfish their shape. It's palace beneath the sea is called Ryugu.

Sui-ryu: This is one of the Japanese Dragon Kings. It has attained the full maturity of dragonkind and is in charge of all the rains. For this it is also known as the Rain Dragon.

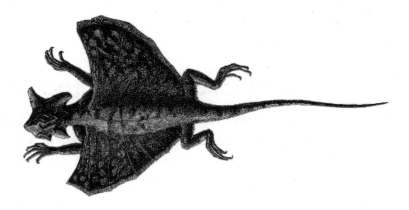

Flying Dragon

Ukasima Dragon: This is a great white-scaled dragon that dwells in the Ukasima Lake at Yama-shiro, near Kyoto. It is said that every 50 years the dragon ascends from the lake and takes the form of a golden songbird, or o-goa-cho. The dragon's songs, however, bring only sadness and misery to the land and are reminiscent of the mournful sound of wolfsong. The sight or sound of this creature is a portent of disaster and ill fortune. The Ukasima Dragon is usually a herald for severe drought. The last reported sighting of the o-goa-cho was in April of 1834. Widespread famine and an outbreak of the plague followed this last sighting of the Ukasima Dragon.

Uwibami: A huge dragon that delighted in attacking people from the sky and dragging them off their horses. Uwibami was defeated by the warrior Yegara-no-Heida.

Yamata Dragon: This hydraesque dragon had eight heads and eight tails. Some Asian dragons were prone to act like their European kin, as was this one. It was known for kidnapping and eating people along the Koshi road (this dragon also bears the name Koshi Dragon). It was defeated by Susawono. The Yamata Dragon is one of the dragon cards in the popular card game *Yu-Gi-Oh*.

Yofune-Nushi: While this dragon appeared to be an Asiatic dragon, its actions were more in keeping with European dragons. It was a mean, vicious dragon who required sacrifice to placate it and quiet its terrible fury, not unlike the Yamata Dragon.

Middle Eastern and Asian Dragons

Many other Asiatic cultures feature dragons in their myths and lore. The dragons of other Asian countries may be more Western in both nature and appearance than the dragons in Chinese and Japanese myths. They may have four legs, bat-like wings, and a stockier build (typical of Western style dragons), or they may be more like the wurms of the west, giant serpents with dragonesque heads.

Types of Dragons

Ananta: This hydra of Hindu mythology had a serpent's body and 1,000 heads. Ananta (also called Sesha or Shesha the Endless) creates amrita, the elixir of immortality, by churning up the ocean. The god Vishnu sleeps upon the massive serpent's back.

Ananta

Asdeev: This white dragon of Persian myth resembles a Western style dragon with four legs and bat-like wings. Asdeev was slain by the warrior, Rustam.

Azhdaha: In ancient Persia (in the land now called Iran), these dragons were believed to be the guardians of all the ganj, or subterranean treasures of the earth. Sound familiar? These dragons are much like the Fu-T'sang-Lung of China.

Azhi Dahaki: One of the greatest of the Persian dragons was Azhi Dahaki (also known as Az Dahak or Azhi Dahaka). This dragon was created by Angra Mainyu, the "father of lies," in an effort to rid the world of righteousness. Azhi Dahaki's body is thought to be filled with all kinds of

poisonous creatures such as spiders, vipers, and scorpions. When the end of the world comes, Azhi Dahaki will break free of its bonds and will devour a third of all the people and animals that dwell on Earth before it is finally subdued. Azhi Dahaki is often depicted as a three-headed, winged serpent. Azi Dahaka dragons make an appearance in the game *Final Fantasy X.*

Buru: A drake of the Himalayas, it has a triangular head with four prominent fangs. At roughly 15 feet long, its body is covered in armor plating and its stubby legs have powerful claws. The buru is a shy animal that keeps far away from people.

Cynoprosopi: These dragons are akin to the ying-long of China. They are covered with shaggy fur, have dog-like heads, muzzles with profuse beards, and bat-like wings.

Dhrana: This is a mighty seven-headed hydra of Indian myth. This dragon was the king of serpents and the guardian of the god Parsva.

Ganj: This dragon is built similar to Western dragons such as Asdeev. Ganj is a huge dragon and the guardian of a massive horde that includes gold, silver, gems, and jewels of all types, as well as mystical artifacts. Ganj has a dragon jewel embedded in his forehead.

Kaliya: A hydra of Indian myth, Kaliya was once the King of Serpents. He is bejeweled and has five heads, two less than his successor.

Kinabalu: This dragon lived on Mount Kinabalu in Borneo. It was a grand dragon with shimmering blue scales. Kinabalu was the keeper of a beautiful Pearl of Wisdom, sought after by the Chinese Emperor.

Leongalli: A Mongolian dragon with a serpentine body, a lion head, and lion forequarters.

Leviathan: The Jewish Talmud calls this great creature the "dragon of the sea." The Leviathan is a huge beast that is able to breathe fire. Originally God created two Leviathan, a male and a female. However, God realized that if allowed to breed, the Leviathan and their descendents would wipe out everything else in the sea. God destroyed one of the Leviathan and as a repayment, He made the remaining one immortal.

Leviathan

Makara: The makara is a type of Indian dragon that has both elephantine and crocodilian traits. This dragon is primarily a water dwelling creature.

Mang: These Korean dragons resemble the Chinese kioh-lung and ying-lung. The mang are a symbol of temporal power.

Naga: These are dragons of India. They usually have serpent bodies with human-like heads, and may have wings and/or two limbs. They can shapeshift into a full serpent form or into a human form. Some naga of note are Apala, Apalala, Musilindi, and Takshaka.

Odontotyrannus: An enormous drake that lived along the River Ganges. It was covered in black scales and sported three huge horns on its head. An odontotyrannus attacked Alexander and the Macedonian army, killing many soldiers.

The Seven: These are the Dragon Gods of the Dun'marra. Each of the Seven corresponds to one of seven Elements. **Grael the Black** is a great black dragon with ruby-red eyes, feathery wings, curling ram horns over horse-like ears, and a furry mane. She also has tufts of fur at her ankles and elbows. Her body is long and slinky and her muzzle is narrow and tapered. She has barbels like a Chinese dragon. Grael is known as the Lady Wardragon and is tied to Chaos. **Ayahz the White**, the Master Healer, has the same body build as his mate Grael. However, Ayahz has leathery wings rather than feathered ones, pearly white scales, and blue eyes. He is tied to Order. Bahamut is the son of Grael and Ayahz. **Bahamut the Silver** is the Lord of Time. He is built in the more stocky form of Western style dragons and has silver-grey scales and horns on his head. **Freyeth the Flame Lord** belongs to the Element of Fire. This dragon is dark reddish-orange. He is built as the Western dragons are, and has jet black horns on his head, fiery orange eyes, leathery wings, and a black mane running down his back. **Gaia the Mother Earth Dragon**, has the slinky, serpentine build of Asian dragons. She is scaled in emerald green with brown eyes. Gaia does not have wings and sports only stubby horns on her head. She is associated with the Element of Earth. **Rai the Thunder Lord** is a serpentine dragon with blue-gray feathered scales. He has only two hind limbs with bird-like feet and wings that are feathered. His head is crocodilian and sports a feather crest. Rai is tied to the Element of Air. **Tiama'at, the Mistress of all Waters**, is a wingless, limbless dragon scaled in blue. She lives in the oceans and controls all of the waters of the planet.

Vritra: The limbless Vritra was the mortal enemy of the god Indra. This wurm was said to hold all of the waters of the heavens in its belly.

Dragons in Europe

Dragons are a very common theme in European myth and legend. Vikings painted dragons on their shields and carved dragon heads on the prows of their longships. Dragons are especially prominent in heraldry. The **heraldic dragon** is most often associated with King Arthur. The **Arthurian dragon** has four legs; ribbed, bat-like wings; the belly of a crocodile; eagle talons; and a serpentine tail. The **heraldic wyvern** looks much like the Arthurian dragon, only lacking the front legs. Other heraldic dragons have a wolf-like head, the body of a serpent, eagle talons, bat-like wings, and a barbed tongue and tail. While dragons were used as the emblem of some of the Roman cohorts, dragons as heraldic creatures did not become overly popular until the age of the Tudors.

In earlier times, most European dragons were actually symbolic of good things, similar to their Asian cousins. However, in Medieval times the dragon became symbolic of all things evil. It represented the devil, hell, sin, darkness, destruction, war, and greed. In the Middle Ages, during the Festival of the Rogotian (which preceded Ascension Day), an image or statue of a dragon was carried around the village as a representation of evil and sin. On the last three days of the festival, the dragon image was kicked around and stoned by the villagers as a way of ridding themselves of evil and sin.

Dragons are an important part of Arthurian myth and legend. Some people believed the heraldic dragon originated with King Arthur. The King's last name (Pendragon) means "head of the dragon," and it is said that Arthur's golden helm resembled a dragon's head.

There were many different types of dragons among the European countries, and quite often they lend their names to cities, as in the case of Worms, Drachenfell, Drakeford, Drakeshill, Draguignan, and many others.

Types of Dragons

Agathodemon: A winged serpent of Grecian myth; it is associated with good luck.

Aiatar: A Finnish wyrm also called the "Devil of the Woods." The children of Aiatar, who take the form of small snakes, cause sickness and disease to all who see them.

Aitvaras: A Lithuanian dragon that can shapeshift into a black cat. It was seen by some as a source of good luck and by others as a demonic being. The aitvaras would attach itself to a family or person and bring good luck and fortune to the household. Unfortunately, many people viewed association with the aitvaras as a form of sorcery or Witchcraft.

Alicha: The great cosmic dragon of Siberian myth, the alicha had huge, black wings. It was said that the alicha had spread its wings if the day was cloudy and overcast. Markings on the moon are said to have been caused by the alicha's claws.

Amphisbaena: These are serpent-dragons having a head at each end! The name is Greek for "go both ways" and supposedly the creature would stick one head inside the mouth of the other and simply roll its way to wherever it wanted to go. Sometimes the amphisbaena was depicted as having feet, but most often it was in the form of a serpent-dragon. Pliny records some medicinal uses of the amphisbaena, such as wearing a live

Amphisbaena

specimin as protection for pregnant women, or wearing a dead one as a cure for rheumatism.

Amphiteres: A legless, winged serpent with a dragonesque head, usually found in Wales and England. It has eyes that resemble a peacock's tail and wings that sparkle or glitter. The wings may be feathered or bat-like. Amphiteres are 6 to 9 feet long and covered in heavy scales. Amphiteres may also be found in many other cultures. Perhaps the most well-known actually come from Mesoamerica. These are the plumed serpent gods Kulkulcan and Quetzalcoatl.

Arassas: Reminiscent of the Tatzelwurm, this creature dwelt in the French Alps. It had a dragonesque body and the head of a cat.

Beithir: A great wurm of Scottish myth; the Beithir was scaled in black with fiery red eyes. It lives among the mountains of Glen Coe.

Bistern Dragon: This classical dragon terrorized Hampshire, England in the 16th century. It is said that a knight, Sir Moris Berkeley, took his hunting hounds and went to confront the dragon. Unfortunately, Sir Moris and his hounds perished in the attempt. Berkeley's family crest and coat of arms were changed to reflect the knight's heroic deed.

Carthiginian Serpent: The Roman army confronted this giant serpent dragon along the Bagrada River. It was 120 feet long and dwelled in the river itself. The serpent was slain by the army and the skin of the giant beast was kept in the temple on Capitol Hill until 133 B.C., after which it disappeared.

Cetus: This great sea serpent of Greek myth belonged to the sea god Poseidon. It was limbless, with coils of ocher and aquamarine. Cetus had a head like that of a hound, with two walrus tusks protruding from the jaws. While it lacked true limbs, it did have vestigal, membranous flippers along its torso. Most striking of all was the fiery red crest that surrounded Cetus's head.

Classical Dragon

Chudo-Yudo: This Russian hydra was thought to be a descendant of Baba Yaga. Chudo-Yudo had the power to control the weather and was often beseeched for good weather and help with crops.

Cirein Croin: These great sea serpents of Scottish myth are so large that they can swallow whales whole. They have grayish scales and a great crest upon their heads. Indeed, the cirein croin's name means "Grey Crest."

Classical Dragons: These dragons are the ones most often used in heraldry. They are the ferocious, fire-breathing enemies of knights

European Sea Serpent

ferocious, fire-breathing enemies of knights and heros. The classical dragons have impenetrable scales covering their bodies, four powerful limbs ending in eagle-like talons, bat-like wings, and long tails that often ended in spikes or stings.

Dragonet: These little dragons are built like the classical dragons, but are less than three feet high. Nevertheless, they are hostile to people and very territorial. The most famous and well-known dragonets are the Wilser, who dwell on the Swiss Mount Pilate. A dragonet could breathe poison breath and their blood was caustic to anything with which it came in contact.

Dragon Whales: These are dragons with whale-like bodies, four flippers, and long serpentine necks culminating in a dragonesque or crocodilian head. Sound familiar? These dragons were likely dinosaurs of the plesiosaur family. The most well-known dragon whale today is Nessie of Loch Ness fame. In nearby Loch Morag another dragon whale dwells.

Firedrakes: Similar to their cousins the icedrakes, firedrakes look like overgrown lizards. These dragons breathe fire, just as their name suggests. They have red to reddish-orange scales, and can be anywhere from 20 to 80 feet in length. Like the icedrakes, firedrakes keep treasure hoards. A firedrake was slain by the warrior Beowulf in the epic poem of the same name. Firedrakes are found in many of the *Final Fantasy* and other computer role-play gaming (RPG) games.

Guivre: Also known as the gargouille, this dragon is the French variant of the wurms. They are associated with woodlands, rivers, streams, and deep wells. The guivre is especially toxic. Wherever one dwells, so also dwells death and destruction. On an interesting note, the mere sight of a naked human is enough to scare the wits out of the gargouille.

Hydra: A dragon with many heads, the hydra usually lacks wings, though some may have them. Oftentimes they have no feet at all. In many stories featuring hydra, when one head is cut off, another grows in its place. Sometimes, two or more heads will replace the one cut off. Two famous Hydra are the hydra of Lernea and the Apocalyptic Beast. Hydra show up in the game *Culdcept.*

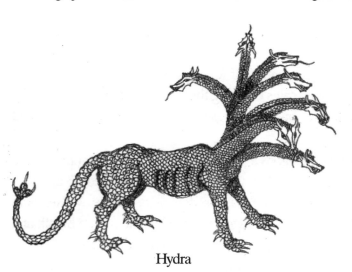

Hydra

Icedrakes: Drakes of any kind resemble classical dragons, but they lack wings. Icedrakes sport white to bluish-gray scales and exhale snow and hail rather than poison breath or fire. Icedrakes are anywhere from 15 to 60 feet in length. As many of the other dragonkin, Icedrakes are fond of treasure and often guard large hoards. Icedrakes are found in many of the *Final Fantasy* and other computer RPG games.

Kashchei: Called Kashchei the Deathless, this serpentine dragon had two legs and two arms. He used an egg as a phylactery for his soul, thus making him immortal—or so he thought. The hero Bulat found the egg and smashed it, killing the dragon.

Knucker: This classical dragon lived in a hole in Lyminster (Sussex, England) and terrorized the locals by eating people and livestock. There are several versions to the folktale of Knucker. In what is perhaps the most well-known version, the king offers his daughter in marriage to anyone who can slay the dragon. A wandering knight slays the dragon and takes the princess as his wife. In another variation, a boy named Jim Puttock bakes a pie full of poison and leaves it as an offering to the dragon. Knucker takes the bait and dies from the poison. In a similar version, a young boy named Jim Pulk bakes the poison pie and leaves it for the dragon. Pulk, however, isn't as lucky as Puttock; he ingests some of the same poison and dies as well.

Lambton Wurm: This wurm had dark black scales and a dragonesque head. It was also a very fat dragon because it ate so much. The Lambton Wurm started life as a small, eel-like creature barely 3 feet long. John Lambton caught it while fishing and threw it into a well. As time passed, the wurm grew in size until it was big enough to coil around a hill seven to nine times.

Lindorm: Also called a lindwurm, this legless serpent sported a pair of bat-like wings and was decked out in brilliant greenish-gold or greenish-silver scales. In the Germanic-Nordic folksagas and Middle High Germanic epic poems, these dragons are often portrayed as the guardians of hidden treasures or damsels in distress. Marco Polo described seeing lindorms while on his travels. According to Polo, they were strong enough and fast enough to take down a man on a galloping horse.

Master Stoorworm: This huge sea serpent of Celtic myth lived by the sea and would devour people and livestock daily. Stoorworm was defeated by a young man named Jamie (or Assipattle) and his teeth formed the Orkney, Shetland, and Faroe Islands. His body became the island of Iceland.

Muirdris: These dragons, also called sinach, are Irish sea serpents of fearsome proportions. They have greenish-blue scales and horns on their heads.

Nessie: The Loch Ness monster, or Nessie, was first sighted in 565 C.E. by Saint Columba as he crossed the loch with a group of followers. Despite her early appearance, Nessie's fame did not become widespread until the 1930s. The first modern sighting occurred in 1933, and they still occur to this day. Nessie is a dragon whale, having a long neck and flippers. As we shall see later dragon whales are believed to be remnants of the plesiosaur family.

Nidhoggr: This dragon of Norse mythology is a dragon of death. It feasts upon the blood and flesh of the dead. Nidhoggr dwells at the base of the Yggdrasil, a giant ash tree, and gnaws at its roots.

Paiste: This huge, 11-foot-long wurm of Irish myth had ram horns that curled around ox-like ears, long fangs full of venom, and ebony, armored scales the size of dinner plates. Paiste was an ancient dragon from the beginning of the world. It was eventually bound to the depths of Loch Foyle by Saint Murrough.

Ollipeist: A type of Irish wurm with glittering, emerald-green scales. An Ollipeist carved out the Shannon Valley.

Ouroboros: Also called oroborus, uroboros, or oureboros, it is the great serpent that bites its own tail. The ouroboros has been dates back to about 1600 B.C. originating in Egypt and moving from there to the Phonecians and on to the Greeks, who made it a popular image. The Norse serpent dragon, Jormungander, is a later representation of the ouroboros. Jormungander lies along the ocean floor, wrapping around the entire Earth, biting her tail in her mouth. The ouroboros is a symbol of life and death, of the Cycle of Nature, and a source of renewal. For the alchemist, the ouroboros is a purifier, and keeps the cosmic waters under control. Here, too the ouroboros

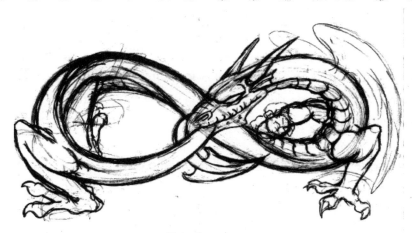

Ouroboros

is representative of the cyclical nature of the alchemist's work. The ouroboros shows up in modern fantasy in the form of the Great Serpent of Robert Jordan's *Wheel of Time* novels.

Sea Serpents: These are sea-dwelling serpent dragons. These dragons move vertically rather than horizontally as true serpents do. They have dragonesque heads and may or may not have horns. Some sea serpents sport the remnants of flippers.

Serpent Dragons: These are the dragons that are more commonly called wurms, wyrms, or worms. They are associated with lakes, rivers, and the sea. They resemble nothing more than huge serpents, being limbless

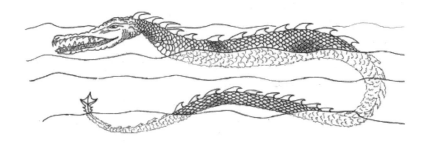

Serpent Dragon

and wingless with a dragonesque head and long crocodilian jaws. Wyrms may or may not sport horns on their heads. However, all of them have a poison breath that killed anything that comes in contact with it. A well known wurm from Norse mythology is Jormungander, the Midgard Wurm.

Serra: This is a sea-dwelling version of the tatzelwurm. It has a long, serpentine body, the head of a lion, and bat wings. These dragons are fond of chasing ships.

Tarasque: This was a classical dragon who dwelled in a lake in France and was prone to devouring virgins. Saint Martha charmed the dragon and led it to the nearest village, where it was slain.

Tatzelwurm: A dragon of the Bavarian, Austrian, and Swiss Alps, it's name means "wurm with claws." It is also called the stollenwurm or hole-dwelling wurm. The tatzelwurm has a long, snake-like body with two clawed forepaws and the head of a cat. Some accounts give the tatzelwurm hind-limbs, while others do not. Likewise, some accounts give it smooth skin, while others feature it having small scales. One of the tatzelwurm's most interesting abilities is that it can jump high and far, earning it the

Tatzelwurm

nickname "springwurm." Similar creatures have been sighted further south than the Alps. The last reported sighting of a stollenwurm was in Palermo, Sicily in 1954.

Winged Serpents: These dragons are snakes with wings. They do not have the dragonesque heads of the amphiteres. Their wings may be feathered or winged and they may have up to four sets of wings, though one is the norm.

Wyvern: A two-legged dragon whose name comes from the French wyvere, which means both "viper" and "life." In its earliest incarnations the wyvern was seen as a protector of the land and a bringer of life. The life-giving aspects of the wyvern have been subverted in some Western cultures (especially after the arrival and domination of Christianity), where it appears in the folklore as a malignant predator. Even it's "Breath of Life" was corrupted and transformed into a poison breath. Most often the wyvern is associated with war, pestilence, and envy. Another French variety of this dragon is the voivre, which is often depicted with the head and upper body of a voluptuous woman, with a ruby or garnet set in the forehead to help guide her through the Underworld or to serve as a healing agent, much like the Carbuncle's ruby.

Dragons of the Americas

What region of the globe do you think of when you hear the word dragon? Probably Europe or China, yes? It never occurs to most people that dragonlore occurs in the Americas with just as great a frequency as it does elsewhere. Dragons are present in large numbers in the Native cultures of the Americas. Think for a moment. Surely you have heard of the Aztec god **Quetzalcoatl**? The great, feathered serpent? Quetzalcoatl and his predecessor, Kulkulcan, are types of dragons similar to the **amphiteres** we saw in European myth. An even older variation of this same feathered dragon is Palulukon.

Dragons of every variety roam the wilds of the Americas. Likely, if you live in the United States, you have dragons in the ancient (or not so ancient!) lore of your home state. And if you live in Central or South America, then your local folklore is likely rife with them!

North America

Amhuluk: This dragon of Oregon myth is a sea serpent with horns on its head. One of the amhuluk's favorite things to do is lure people close to the water and then drown them. The amhuluk is believed to undergo a series of transformations, each one leaving it even more formidable than before. This dragon is associated with thieves, but the reasoning is lost to the past.

The Ancient One: This sea serpent of Piute myth dwells in Lake Pyramid, Nevada. The Ancient One, like the amhuluk, enjoys snagging people from the shore and drowning them. Whenever the Piute see whirlpools in Lake Pyramid they avoid it, as it means the Ancient One is about and looking for victims.

Angont: The angont is a sacred serpent-dragon found in Huron myth. The angont is a viscious and poisonous dragon known for causing disease, illness, and disaster. Indeed, the very flesh of this dragon is poisonous, much like poison dart frogs. The angont lives in desolate places such as caves, wild forests, and the depths of lakes.

Az-I-Wu-Gum-Ki-Mukh-Ti: This dragon of Inuit myth has a walrus-like head, a dog-like body, and dog-like legs/feet, a whale fluke for a tail, and black scales. This immense beast can sink ships with one blow from its tail, and is much feared by Inuit fishermen.

Gaasyendietha: This dragon of Seneca myth is believed to have come from the meteors that fall from the heavens to crash in the earth. For this reason, it is also known as the meteor dragon. The gaasyendietha is a huge dragon that dwells in rivers and lakes. Meteor dragons show up in the popular anime series and card game *Yu-Gi-Oh* as the Meteor Dragon and Black Meteor Dragon, the latter of which is a most powerful creature.

Gloucester's Sea Serpent: This 45 to 55-foot-long beast was reportedly spotted in Boston Harbor. It had a horse-like head and moved as most sea serpents are given to move—more like an inchworm than a snake.

Gowrow: The gowrow is a 20–30 foot long lizard-like creature found in the legends and lore of Arkansas. This dragon has giant tusks protruding from its jaws and is believed to be a subterranean dragon, coming out from caves and fissures to feed. The last recorded sighting of a gowrow was in 1951, in the Ozark Mountains.

Haietlik: This serpent dragon of the Nootka and Clayoqut Indians is called the Lightning Serpent. This dragon has a serpentine body and a horse-like head. Haietlik dwells in the lakes and waterways. Pictograms of the Haietlik adorn the rocks in the area.

Horned Serpents: These dragons can be found all over North America. They are huge serpent dragons sporting one or two horns upon their heads. The horned serpents are gilled water dwellers, however they can also breathe out of water. The horned serpents are the mortal enemies of the Thunderbirds.

Kikituk: This dragon of the Inuit is saurian in appearance. It is a huge creature with four feet, but lacking in wings, much like the European drake.

Horned Serpent

Kolowisi: A dragon of Zuni myth, the Kolowisi is an enormous, water-dwelling serpent dragon with horns adorning its head and fish-like fins in place of feet and hands.

Meshkenabec: This giganitic sea serpent had plate-sized scales of a ruby red color and a wedge-shaped head. Meshkenabec was slain by the warrior Manabozho.

Msi-kinepeikwa: A serpent dragon of Shawnee myth, it also called kinepeikwa. This dragon grows slowly and through metamorphoses, much like its Asiatic brethren. Each transformation takes place by shedding the previous form away, much like a snake sheds its skin or a tarantula sheds its exoskeleton. In the first stage, kinepeikwa is a fawn with one red horn and one blue one. The final transformation leaves behind a massive, lake-dwelling serpent dragon.

Ogopogo: This sea serpent dwells in Canada's Lake Okanagan. It is roughly 70 feet long, with the horse-like head commonly seen in sea serpents. Ogopogo has numerous fins running along its serpentine body.

Piasa: The name Piasa means "destroyer." This dragon is a hodgepodge of animal parts, much like the Asiatic dragons. The Piasa has the head of

Piasa

a bear, the horns of an elk, scales like a fish, and bear's legs with an eagle's claws. The Piasa has a mane around its head and shoulders and sports a tail that is at least 50 feet long and can wrap around its body three times. The Native Americans call this dragon Stormbringer or Thunderer. In 1673, Father J. Marquette saw a rock painting of the Piasa along the Illinois/Mississippi River. This painting was painted in natural blacks, reds, and blues. Unfortunately, in the year 1876, a land developer destroyed the rock sculpture in his greed to build yet more buildings. The current Piasa rock painting located along the Mississippi River near Alton, Illinois is a reconstruction of the one Marquette reported seeing. This 48 x 22 painting is located on a 100 x 75 section of the bluffs.

Pal-rai-yuk: This Alaskan dragon has six legs on a long, snake-like body. Spikes run along the dragon's spine. The pal-rai-yuk lives in the rivers and waters of Alaska, and the Inuit peoples paint its picture on their canoes before using them, to serve as a ward against the fearsome beast's attentions.

Palulukon: These dragons are part of the plumed serpent family of amphiteres along with the dragon gods of Meso-America. They are powerful dragons, but are neither good nor bad. They just are. The palulukon are weather workers and

Pal-rai-yuk

represent the Element of Water. They are in charge of bringing the rains, and it said that the world is carried through the cosmic ocean on the backs of two of these colossal beasts. If mistreated, the palulukon can wreak much damage by unleashing natural disasters such as drying up wells, rivers, and water holes and allowing the rains to cease falling. They may even cause earthquakes.

Polar worms: These are dragons of Inuit legend similar to the wurms of Europe. These were long serpentine creatures with dragonesque heads and ferocious tempers.

Sisiutl: This two-headed supernatural sea serpent has the ability to shapeshift into a self-propelled canoe. To maintain its energy, it has to have a steady diet of seals. He is said to dwell in the Pacific Northwest.

Stvkwvnaya: A dragon of Seminole myth, the stvkwvnaya is also called a tie snake. These dragons are huge serpentine creatures with a single horn sprouting from their foreheads. The horn of the stvkwvnaya, when powdered, was believed to be a powerful aphrodisiac. The only way to get a stvkwvnaya's horn was to summon it and chant to keep the beast calm.

Tatoskok: The tatoskok is a sea serpent that also goes by the more modern designation of Champ. It lives in Lake Champlain, and is believed to be one of the horned serpents by the Abenaki. Tatoskok is roughly 30 feet long with a horse-like head. This sea serpent has been spotted many times over the years and a popular explanation is that like Nessie, it is a remnant of a plesiosaur, basilosaurus, or other prehistoric beast.

Tcipitckaam: Also called the unicorn serpent, this Canadian horned serpent species has a serpentine body, a horse-like head, and a single spiraling horn jutting from its head. It dwells mainly in lakes. Some tcipitckaam have been described as resembling a drake in appearance, having a stockier body and four stubby legs, but still sporting the spiraling horn on its head.

Teehooltsoodi: This dragon of the Navajo is kin to the ying-long of China. It has a slinky, otter-like body and buffalo-like horns on its head. The teehooltsoodi live in rivers and can cause them to overflow.

Uktena: This dragon, found in Tennessee, North Carolina, and South Carolina, resembles a giant serpent. The uktena has the girth of a large tree, with stag horns on its head, giant eagle wings, and scales that gleam similar to fire. It has spots of color all along its body and can only be killed by wounding it at the seventh spot from the head. The uktena sports a gem in its forehead, called an Ulun'suti. This gem, as with the Asiatic dragon pearls, is a source of power. If a man can claim an Ulun'suti he can become a great worker of miracles and wonders. However, to try and seize the gem is a great folly. The uktena's gaze can daze a man and make him run towards the serpent instead of away from it. In addition, the uktena has a poison breath that can kill instantly.

Wakandagi: An unusual dragon of the Mohawk Indians, it is possessed of a long slinky body, a slender tapered muzzle with sharp teeth, deer antlers on its head, and hooves for feet in place of claws.

Meso-America

Chac: This dragon of Mayan myth controls the rains and rules over all the waters. He requires a sacrifice in order for the rains to come, but he repays human sacrifices with his own blood. He has a long, serpentine body scaled like a fish and catfish whiskers at the end of a tapered snout. Stag horns adorn his crocodilian head, as do deer-like ears. Chac is often depicted holding his lightning ax in one paw.

Coatlcue: A dragon of Aztec mythology, Coatlcue represents a woman's fertility and fecundity. She is also known as Chihuacoatl or "Serpent Skirt." Coatlcue is often depicted as a hydraesque creature with a serpentine body and two heads. This form sometimes sports claws and at other times does not. In another form, she is a human-looking female with a necklace of severed human hands and a skirt of writhing serpents. A statue of Coatlcue can be found at La Troba University in Melbourne.

Itzamna: This dragon-god of the Mayans is the son of the Sun god Hunabku. Itzamna is a patron god of doctors, writing, and learning, much as Hermes is to the Greeks and Thoth to the Egyptians.

Kulkulkan: The Mayan equivalent to Quetzalcoatl, this plumed serpent god is a bit bloodthirsty. He requires sacrifice, whereas Quetzalcoatl allowed it to be voluntary.

Lord Nine Winds: This dragon is the Mixtec equivalent to Kulkulkan and Quetzalcoatl. Like the previous Plumed Serpent gods, Lord Nine Winds is an amphitere. He is a creator god as well.

Quetzalcoatl: The Aztec feathered serpent god controls the winds and rains. He is the God of Knowledge and of the finer crafts and arts. Quetzalcoatl is credited with creating the calendar system. Other names for this well-known specimen of the amphitere family are Ehecatl and the Lord of the Dawn. Quetzalcoatl has multicolored scales and feathers. He is often depicted soaring through the sky, creating a rainbow. The serpent god is also known to take the form of a human on occasion. Quetzalcoatl was believed to have departed from this realm for the east, traveling on a raft made from serpents. He will one day return. The Aztecs viewed the coming of Cortez and his Spaniards as the return of the Great Plumed One.

Winged Serpent

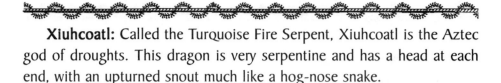

Xiuhcoatl: Called the Turquoise Fire Serpent, Xiuhcoatl is the Aztec god of droughts. This dragon is very serpentine and has a head at each end, with an upturned snout much like a hog-nose snake.

South America

Bachue: Bachue is a dragon goddess of the Chibcha peoples of Colombia. Long ago she emerged from Lake Iguaque in the form of a human. With her, she brought a small boy who she later married and had six children with. Thus they were the progenitors of the human race. Once these humans had grown up and learned to live on their own, Bachue turned her mate and herself into dragons and they returned to the depths of Lake Iguaque, where they still dwell today. Bachue is the goddess of agriculture and the harvest, as well as the goddess of famine.

Faery dragon: Also called fairy dragons, fey dragons, or penny dragons, this type of dragon is prevalent in South America. They range from the size of a mouse to about a foot in length. The faery dragon resembles a classical dragon of Europe in build, but there are several important differences (besides the size, that is!). Penny dragons sport two sets of dragonfly or butterfly wings. They have a longer, more tapered snout; large iridescent eyes; and are colored to blend in with their surroundings in the same manner that moths, butterflies, and other insects do. However, if the light hits them just right, the faery dragon's hide will shine with a rainbow of colors.

Iemisch: This Patagonian dragon is similar to the tatzelwurm of Europe. It has a serpentine body with the forequarters of a fox. The iemisch will use its body to ensnare victims and crush them like a boa or python.

Ihuaivulu: This South American dragon dwells in volcanoes. It has a slinky, serpent body with burnished copper and red scales. The Ihuaivulu is a South American version of the hydra and sports seven heads. As a volcano dweller, it can breathe fire.

Iwanci: A sea serpent from the Ecuadoran Amazon River basin, this dragon is a shapeshifter with two forms. One is Macanci, the water snake. The other is Pani, the anaconda.

Lampalugua: A drake that inhabits Chile, it has dusty-reddish scales and preys upon both livestock and people.

Dragons of Africa and Oceania

The dragons of Africa and Oceania tend to be a hodge-podge of all the dragons we have previously seen. There are amphiteres, horned serpents, drakes, and sea serpents, among others. Dragons in these areas also tend to be both good and bad. Again, a mix of all the ones before. A popular dragon theme of these regions are the **rainbow serpents**. These were often wurms that sported rainbow-hued scales and were associated with rainbows and rain-bringing. Sometimes rainbow serpents fall into the amphitere or winged serpent category.

Africa

Aido Hwedo: This large rainbow serpent of West African myth is said to hold the world together. Much like Jormungander, she rests in the oceans, coiled all the way around the world. It is said that when Aido Hwedo trembles, the earth quakes.

Akhekhu: A drake of Egyptian myth, these dragons are considered semi-supernatural beings. These dragons are long and serpentine, but sport no wings at all.

Ammut: This chimeric dragon is also known as the Eater of the Dead or Eater of Souls. She has a crocodilian head and a furry beast-like body. Ammut waits with Anubis, the jackal-headed god of death, while souls are weighed against the Feather of Truth upon the Scales of Judgment. If a soul's heart does not measure up to the god's strict challenge, then it is consumed by Ammut.

Apep: This Egyptian sea serpent is a symbol of chaos, instability, and eclipses. Unlike most sea serpents, Apep is bulkier in build, being more akin to the ancient saurian Lipleurodon. Apep chases the Sun god Ra through the underworld each night, trying to quench the Sun. Sometimes he swallows the sun, causing an eclipse, but he always regurgitated it.

Bida: A giant wurm of Soniniki myth, this is the dragon who blesses the city of Wagadu with gold in exchange for a sacrifice of 10 maidens per year.

Denwen: A fiery wurm of Egyptian myth, Denwen was shunned by the gods and sought revenge. But the King of Egypt slew him, thus preventing him from harming the gods. Denwen is a symbol of the ultimate evil.

Gandareva: An immense wurm of Sumerian myth, this dragon enjoyed eating people. Gandareva fought many battles against a valient warrior named Keresapa. Keresapa lost 15 horses and his sight to Gandareva, but eventually the worthy hero prevailed.

Humbaba: This dragon of Sumerian and Babylonian myth is a chimeric dragon similar to the Piasa. Humbaba had a body like a lion's, but it was scaled all over like a snake. On his head were two bull-like horns and his feet sported vulture-like claws. This fierce dragon was the guardian of the forests. Humbaba appears in the Epic of Gilgamesh where he is eventually slain by Gilgamesh, with the assistance of Enkidu. Humbaba appear in the *Final Fantasy* game series, often as greater forms of the Behemoth enemies. They also show up in the game *Culdcept*.

Kongamato: This dragon is a wyvern of Zambia. It is a small dragon with a wingspan of only 3-4 feet and a tapered muzzle full of sharp teeth. It is covered in leathery reddish-brown skin. Living in the Jiundu swamps, its favorite pastime is swooping down and capsizing boats.

Kur: This Sumerian dragon angered the gods and Ninurta, son of Ehlil, was ordered to eliminate him. When Kur was destroyed, a great flood of dirty water was released. Ninurta piled rocks upon the great beast's body to dam the water. Then Ninurta led the people to the Tigris River so that they could rebuild.

Mehen: This giant, golden wurm is a guardian of Ra and of the Sun Boat. Often he is depicted as being coiled around the Sun Boat while Ra stands in the center.

Mokolo-Mbembe: This is the name given to a drake living in the Congo region. This dragon is semi-aquatic and sports a long slender tail and equally slender neck.

Nguma-monene: This giant wurm of the Congo has a rigid crest running the length of its back. It is said to make its home in the Dongou-Mataba River.

Nebuchadnezzar's Dragon: This dragon of Babylonian myth was long and serpentine. Covered in burnished, sand-colored scales, this dragon sported crests on its neck and horns on its head. King Nebuchadnezzar kept this dragon in the temple until Daniel killed it with poison to prove that it was not a god and not worthy of worship.

Nehebkau: This drake has a long slinky body and human-like hands and legs. Nehebkau is tamed by Ra and often rides with him in the Sun Boat. He is immune to Water, Fire, and a handful of other magicks. Nehebkau's image is often used as a ward against serpent and scorpion poisons.

Ninki Nanki: This is another Congolese drake. This one has a blunter head, a shorter, sturdier neck and horns on its head. It is known to have a bad temper and to harm people.

Tiamat: Hailing from Assyrio-Babylonian mythology, the great sea dragon Tiamat is the mate of Apsu. Together, Tiamat and Apsu created all the varied gods and goddesses.

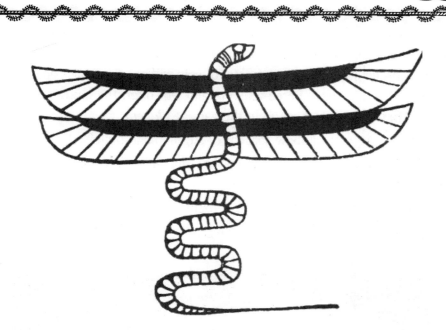

Wadjet

Wadjet: This female dragon is a winged serpent in the form of a cobra. Wadjet has flame breath, said to be as hot as the sun. She is a symbol of royalty and rulership. Images of her appear on the crowns of the Pharaohs.

Oceanía

Aranda: This sea serpent of the Emianga region hides in the deeps of the rivers and swallow up people who came out to fish.

Bobbi-bobbi: This rainbow serpent took one of his own ribs to create the first boomerang so that people could hunt the animals of the earth for food.

Bunyip: These chimeric dragons of Australia are as old in myth as the rainbow serpents. Most often these dragons are huge serpents with long, oversized ears. Bunyip are credited with being masterful shapeshifters and often choose to take on appearances that they find amusing. Thus we have bunyip that look like giant versions of existing Australian animals and fanciful chimeric creatures made up of many different animal parts. These dragons prefer swamp lands as home. Bunyip will not shy away from eating people. They also have fierce tempers and will flood the lands when angered. These dragons show up in the game *Culdcept*.

Galeru: A giant rainbow serpent of Armhenland beliefs.

Hotu-puku: Another famous taniwha, this one attacks people traveling from Rotorua and Taupo.

Julunggul: This female rainbow serpent is eternally pregnant. She produces the Sisters of Dreamtime. Julunggul can transform from female to

male and back again as desired. Other names for this dragon include: Mumuna, Kalwadi, and Kungpipi.

Kakuru: This large wurm is one of the many rainbow serpents of Australia. This dragon brings the rainbows and is a herald of the coming of the rainy season.

Kataore: This taniwha also caused a disturbance near Rotorua. He was slain by the dragon hunter Pitaka.

Marakihau: These female sea serpents often turn into human females in order to attract and marry human males.

Rainbow Serpent: There are many rainbow serpents, and all are considered gods and sport horns and multicolored scales. They are long, serpentine creatures, often regarded as being the creators of waterways.

Taniwha: These dragons inhabit the deep waters of oceans and rivers. They are rather violent-tempered creatures.

Tarrotarro: This Australian drake is regarded as an ancestor spirit. It is said that Tarrotarro separated the first people into males and females. He also bestowed upon the people the art of tattooing.

Tuteporoporo: A well-known taniwha, Tuteporoporo lived in the Whanguanui River. This dragon was a pet of one Chief Tuariki. Unfortunately Tuteporoporo turned feral, began eating people, and eventually had to be slain.

Warramunga: This male rainbow serpent is a creator god and a symbol of the springtime. One special thing to note about this rainbow dragon is that he is blind. As he flies from waterhole to waterhole he creates rainbows. Another name for Warramunga is Wollunqua.

Yurlunger: This male rainbow serpent is known as the Great Father and, similar to the warramunga, was a creator god. He is a symbol of the ritual changing of boy to man and of fertility. His voice sounds like thunder.

Chapter 2

Dragon Myths of the World

Dragon's Dawn

Roaring fills the air,
reverberating through the night.
Distant roaring echoes the first.
Dragons call to one another.

Reverberating through the night,
deep and calming are these ancient voices.
Dragons, calling to one another,
singing out in the cool night air.

Deep and calming are the dragons' voices,
full of wisdom and strength.
They sing out in the cool night air,
joining together in harmonious melody.
Full of wisdom and the strength of ages,
dragonsong fills the air.
They join together in harmonious melody,
awakening into being a new day.

Dragonsong fills the air,
music of ages past.
The dragons awaken a new day into being.
Guardians of night and day, of past and present.

Music of ages past.
Timeless is the dragons' roaring song.
Guardians of night and day, of past and present.
Creatures as ageless as the world itself.

Timeless is the dragons' roar,
voice of the gods themselves.
Dragons—ageless as the world.
Heralds of a new day.

Voice of the gods themselves,
that is the dragons' song.
Herald to a new day.
Roaring fills the air.

The Legend of Master Stoorworm

Master Stoorworm was a giant sea serpent who resided in the sea near a coastal town. Master Stoorworm had a great appetite, and each morning he would yawn seven times. With each great yawn his mouth would open wider and wider. On the seventh yawn, his mouth would open widest and his long, snake-like tongue would roll out and pull in seven things for him to eat: cattle, chickens, cows, men, women, children, dogs, cats, and so on. It mattered not to Master Stoorworm.

King Harald finally got fed up with the sea serpent's marauding ways, and he called a meeting to decide what should be done. The consensus was to appease the beast by offering him seven maidens on a certain schedule, in the hopes that he would leave them alone for the rest of the time and hunt for himself in the seas. But King Harald did not want to sacrifice his people to the beast. He wanted the dragon dead, and so he promised his daughter's hand in marriage to the one who slew Master Stoorworm. Many answered the call, but most were scared away by the serpent's vile breath. After many failures, and with the dragon still on the rampage, the King ordered a boat to be made so that he could go to battle for himself, for he would rather do that than force the sacrifice of his subjects.

In this town was a young boy name Jamie (or Assipattle in some versions) who was small, yet exceedingly courageous. After all the warriors who had come to the king's challenge were either scared away or dead, Jamie planned to venture out and try his own luck against the beast. During the night he snuck out carrying an iron pot full of peat. He made his way to the docks and there stole the King's boat, rowing out to sea to wait for Master Stoorworm to awaken. With the sea serpent's first great yawn, Jamie's boat was swept down his gullet. He paddled down into the beast's body until he reached the liver. There he used his peat pot to set the liver on fire. As the dragon writhed in agony, Jamie traveled back up the body and out the mouth.

Master Stoorworm struggled and writhed. As he flailed about, his teeth started falling out. These dragon teeth eventually formed Orkney, Shetland, and Faroe Islands. After Stoorworm died, his carcass shriveled up and floated away to later become Iceland.

Beowulf and the Firedrake

Beowulf, after becoming the King of the Geats, fought a legendary battle against a great firedrake. Earlier, someone had found the great drake's cave and snuck in while the dragon slept; treasure was stolen and the culprit fled. It is well known that dragons know every ounce and gem of their treasure hoards, and so, as soon as he awoke, the firedrake knew that his hoard had been violated and treasures stolen. There were human footprints and human-smell in and around his cave, so the mighty dragon knew exactly what had become of his treasure.

Enraged, the fierce dragon began terrorizing the countryside to punish the vile humans for their trespass. Envoys were sent to Beowulf to tell him of the drake's depredations, and to beg that he come and slay the marauder. The Great King Beowulf agreed. He and his entourage traveled to the dragon's lands, but in the end, only one man stood with the King against the dragon. King Beowulf and the drake both fought valiantly, one with sword and shield, the other with claws, teeth, and flaming breath. During the epic conflict Beowulf's sword, Naegling, broke, and Beowulf was bitten by the firedrake. He did not die right away though, and lived long enough to see the dragon die with the help of Wiglaf, one of his relatives. Unfortunately, Beowulf died soon after of his injuries.

Saint George and the Dragon

Because medieval theology turned the dragon into a creature of evil and a symbol of the devil, it makes sense that many saints are slayers of dragons. These include Saint Phillip the Apostle, Saint Romain, Saint Keyne of Cornwall, Saint Clement of Metz, Saint Floret, Saint Cado, Saint Maudet, and Saint Paul. All the stories that pitted the saints against dragons were designed to show Christianity's power over evil. Of course, no collection of medieval folk legends about dragon slayers would be complete without the most famous of all—Saint George.

St. George was born in Turkey some 1,700 years ago. He was a Roman soldier of the Imperial Guard. However, when the Emperor declared that all Christians should be killed, George became horrified and fled the country. He took up the Christian faith for himself, donned a shining suit of armor adorned with a cross on the buckle and shield, and set off to spread the word of Christianity.

Meanwhile, in another region, a huge dragon had

St. George and the Dragon

emerged from the swamps of the Silene and terrorized the land. The enormous dragon, decked out in shimmering green scales, also sported massive wings and a long, curly tail. At first the dragon's hunger and bloodlust was slaked by the sacrifice of two sheep a day. Gradually though, it became necessary to sacrifice a child each day to stave off the dragon's wrath. Months passed in this way, until it was the King's turn to sacrifice his own flesh and blood. The King could not refuse to take part in the ritual that he and his people had perpetuated. His daughter found herself waiting for the dragon, when a tall knight came wandering by. This handsome knight was wearing silver armor emblazoned with a scarlet cross. The knight was none other than George himself. George untied the princess, heard her story, and then waited to meet the dragon for himself.

The dragon came to devour his usual sacrifice only to find himself confronted by Saint George. George and the dragon fought. On and on they fought, until the dragon brought forth its secret weapon. Two seemingly shapeless and useless lumps along its back sprang to life, unfurling to reveal numerous eyes. George could no longer see the dragon, blinded as he was. He threw his lance straight into the seething mass of eyes. The lance struck and the eyes disappeared. The lance had mortally wounded the great beast in its neck. Shrouding it were its huge wings, resplendent with eyespots. This was the source of George's illusion. In return for slaying the dragon, the King allowed George to baptize himself and all of his followers, converting them to Christianity.

Another version of the Saint George legend has George untying the princess, then going to the dragon's lair to confront it. In this version, George fights with the dragon and wounds it badly by plunging his lance into its side. The dragon, exhausted, stops fighting and George tells the princess to tie her silken handkerchief about its neck. The pair led the subdued beast back to the town. The people of Silene killed the dragon, and the King and all of his followers converted to Christianity. In this version

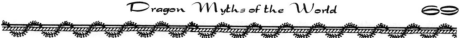

George also marries the King's daughter. According to history, George was later tortured and killed for his beliefs. It was not until 800 years later, when Christianity truly began to flower, that George was named a saint.

Saint Romain and the Gargouille

In the year A.D. 520, the ancient capital of Normandy, Rouen, was under seige by a beast from the Seine. This creature had a snake-like body and neck, a slender head with slender jaws, membranous fins, and eyes that glowed like moonstones. The dragon came ashore, and opening its mouth, spewed forth a mighty torrent of water to flood the countryside. The people dubbed the dragon a gargouille, meaning "gargler," for it's ability to spew forth jets of water. It continued its watery assault until all the land was devastated, the crops ruined, and many people dead.

Saint Romain, the archbishop of Rouen decided that he would confront the beast at its lair and kill it. With him he took a prisoner who was convicted of murder and sentenced to death. This prisoner had nothing to lose by going with Germain; either way he was doomed to death. The pair made their way to the dragon's home and it slithered up to greet them, mouth agape, ready to release a waterspout. Romain, with his hands

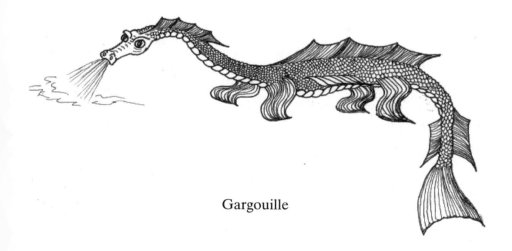

Gargouille

held high, used his fingers to make a cross. Upon seeing this, the gargouille sank down, subdued, and allowed Romain to slip a rope around its neck, whereupon the prisoner led it into town.

The townspeople immediately fell upon the dragon and set it on fire. They disposed of the ashes and remains of the dragon by dumping them into the beast's former home, the River Seine. It is said that many a gargoyle gets its apperance and waterspouting job from the gargouille. Certainly the name gargoyle is derived from gargouille. And what of the prisoner you might ask? Well, he was pardoned for his crimes because he played a role in helping to subdue the dragon. From that day forward, each Ascension Day, the archbishop of Rouen would pardon one prisoner.

The Lambton Wurm

On the morning of Easter Sunday, in the year 1420, John Lambton was fishing in the river near Lambton Castle when he caught what appeared to be some kind of small, elongated eel creature with black, shiny skin and a dragonesque head. It also sported long slender jaws full of needle sharp teeth and eyes that glowed like coals. Disgusted by the little beast, Lambton threw it into one of the castle wells. After seeing the rather disturbing creature, Lambton became a changed man. Fearing he had seen an incarnation of the Devil, he sought redemption and salvation. Lambton set out on a pilgrimmage to the Holy Land in the hopes that he would find what he was looking for.

Meanwhile, back at Lambton Castle, the eel thrived in its new home and grew to enormous proportions. Eventually it escaped the well and took up residence on a nearby hill. The dragon (for a dragon it truly was), grew until it was large enough to wrap around the hill several times. Vapor from its mouth wilted all the grass and trees, leaving the hill dry and barren.

The wurm set about devouring livestock, and even children when it could snag them.

People tried to placate the dragon by setting out troughs of milk in Lambton Court. A routine was started, whereby the villagers would set out an offering of milk each day for the wurm. This kept the beast happy and drowsing on its hill, where it did not attack anyone. A few people did attempt to slay the beast, but the worm always healed and parts would grow back, leaving a very angry wurm. The milk offering pacified the animal for a time, but eventually it grew restless, and when no further offerings of milk were laid out, it began terrorizing the people again.

John Lambton finally came home from his pilgrimage and discovered what had become of his catch. He figured that it was his responsibility to destroy the beast. Lambton sought out the advice of a Witch, asking her how to slay the dragon. She told him that he must don a specially crafted suit of armor with blades covering every surface. Furthermore, he must confront the dragon in the middle of the river from whence it came. Finally, he must kill the next living thing he met after slaying the dragon. If he failed in any of this, then the Lambton line would be cursed, and for nine generations no Lambton heir would live to see old age. Lambton did as he was instructed. He had the armor specially made with blades covering every surface. He managed to lure the dragon back to the river from which he had caught it. Lambton fought the mighty wurm and thanks to his bladed armor, he won the battle. He made his way back home, thinking that his dog would be the first thing to greet him, as it had so often. However, it was his father and not his dog who first greeted him. Lambton couldn't bring himself to kill his own father and so the Lambton line was cursed from then on. Nine generations of Lambton men died tragic deaths.

Siegfried and Fafnir

Siegfried, the stepson of King Alf of Denmark, yearned for what all young men yearn for: fame and glory. Siegfried was somewhat naïve, and was tricked by the dwarf Regin into going to Gnithead to confront the dragon Fafnir, who guarded a vast and wondrous treasure.

Regin agreed to accompany Siegfried and further, he agreed to reforge Siegfried's father's broken sword, Gram. The sword was reforged and the pair set out for Gnithead. However, all was not as it seemed. Regin was a greedy sort, and he only wanted Siegfried to do the hard work in getting the dragon's hoard. Regin intended to kill Sigfried if he was able to slay Fafnir. In truth, Fafnir was Regin's brother. Like Regin, Fafnir had been a greedy sort and had killed their father for the treasure. But Fafnir was cursed. Because he had the lust of a dragon for treasure, he was turned into a dragon as penance for his horrible deed.

Fafnir

For a long time, thoughts of the treasure had lingered and festered in Regin's mind. He was bound and determined to get the dragon's treasure, but because he was small he needed a great warrior's help. All of his previous warriors had perished to the dragon's wrath. This time, though, he had higher hopes. In addition to reforging the mighty sword, Gram, he had coached Siegfried on how to deal with Fafnir. The great dragon's magnificent scales protected his whole body. The only place he was vulnerable was on his underbelly. Siegfried and Regin decided to lay a trap for the dragon. They dug a hole along the path that the dragon took to get to the river. Siegfried hid himself in the hole and let Regin cover the trap so that nothing was amiss. Siegfried remained hidden there, waiting for the dragon to pass by. When the great dragon finally passed over, Siegfried took the opportunity to plunge Gram deep into the dragon's belly. The wound Siegfried inflicted upon Fafnir was a mortal one, and the dragon soon perished.

Once the dragon was dead, Regin came out from his hiding place. He cut open Fafnir and pulled out the heart. He asked that Siegfried cook the heart over the fire, so that Regin could eat it. Thinking nothing of it, Siegfried did as he was asked. He roasted the heart and at one point, he touched it to see if it was done. The hot flesh burned his finger, so to soothe it Siegfried stuck it in his mouth. As soon as he did, he was able to hear the voices of the animals as if they spoke the human tongue. He happened to overhear two birds talking about Fafnir's heart and Regin's plans for Siegfried. Siegfried learned that Regin intended to kill him once he had consumed the dragon heart. Siegfried decided to take the initiative, and he slew the evil dwarf first. He then consumed the heart, gaining all the dragon's power. He went into the dragon's cave to claim the treasure. (Unbeknownst to him, the curse as well.)

Jormungander, the Midgard Wurm

This giant serpent dragon, spawn of the Norse god Loki, was thrown into the ocean by Odin. She wrapped herself around the Earth, biting her tail in her mouth. Here she would remain, for the most part, until Ragnarok and her final confrontation with Thor.

Jormungander and Thor came in contact twice before the final battle. The first happened when Thor chanced to visit Utgardhaloki, the king of the giants. The King challenged Thor to complete three tasks of physical prowess. The first was to pick up the king's cat. Thor tried and tried, but he could not pick it up. Now, what Thor didn't know is that the "cat" was really Jormungander in disguise, and he had actually managed to pull up the head/tail of the great serpent just a bit!

The second encounter between Thor and Jormungander came one day when Thor and his friend, the giant Hymar, were out fishing. Thor was using an oxhead as bait and, as chance would have it, they were near Jormungander's head. She let loose her tail and took the bait. The dragon and Thor fought for what seemed like ages, with neither giving any ground. But as with any fight, one must tire sooner than the other. The great dragon tired before the thunder lord did, and Thor pulled her huge head out of the water, preparing to deliver the deathblow. Unfortunately, Hymar lost his nerve at seeing Jormungander in the flesh. He cut Thor's line, freeing the massive serpent. When Ragnarok finally arrived, Thor and Jormungander met for the final time. Long did this battle last, even as the last one had. Finally, though, Thor landed a fierce blow on the great dragon's head. But Thor lost, in that epic battle. As she lay dying, Jormungander breathed her deadly breath over him, asphyxiating him.

The Mordiford Wyvern

There was once a child named Maud who liked to wander in the woods. One day, Maud came upon a strange animal lying on the forest floor. The creature was about a foot long and had iridescent scales and wings that were folded along its back. The tiny creature took flight at Maud's approach. However, Maud was persistent and patient, and she finally coaxed the little animal to come to her, enticing it with bowls of milk. The baby wyvern curled up in Maud's lap and fell fast asleep.

Unaware of the true nature of her new pet, Maud took the wyvern home with her. When her parents saw what she had brought home, her father ordered her to take it back to where she had found it. Maud, though, did what every child does at least once in his or her life. She didn't take the wyvern back to the forest. Instead, she hid the dragon from her parents and fed it until it was old enough to begin hunting for itself. At first the wyvern only hunted things such as rabbits, squirrels, and birds. But as it grew bigger it needed more and

Mordiford Wyvern

more food. It moved up to hunting sheep and cattle. Then, one fateful day, it killed a shepherd boy and developed a taste for human flesh.

After realizing what easy prey humans were, the wyvern began hunting humans almost exclusively. People began to shun going outdoors, fearing for their lives. Indeed, the only person safe from the deprivations of the dragon was Maud, because she was the one who had played with it and taken care of it when it was younger. Soon even Maud was terrified of her erstwhile pet due to its bloodthirsty hunger.

All attempts to kill the dragon were met with failure. One day a prisoner named Garston offered to try his luck in exchange for his freedom. Garston was condemned to die already, so facing the dragon wasn't too bad of an option. Garston asked that a barrel be made, laced with wicked spikes and blades on the outside. He was placed in the barrel, given a pistol and a sword, then put in a location the wyvern was sure to pass. Eventually, the wyvern passed through the area and smelled human flesh. Being hungry as usual, the dragon tracked the smell to its source. It found Garston's barrel and immediately coiled around it, trying with all its strength to crack the barrel open. The harder the wyvern squeezed the barrel, the more damage it did to itself. Finally, the barrel began to give a bit and started to crack. At this point Garston used the pistol to shoot out of a small peephole in the barrel. This further injured the dragon and it soon collapsed and died, its coils loosening from the barrel. Garston emerged, intent on using the sword to sever the dragon's head. Unfortunately the already dying dragon chose that moment to exhale its last breath, covering him in a toxic cloud. Both convict and dragon perished in the conflict.

Regulus and the Carthiginian Serpent

Most creatures have a basis in fact, and dragons are no exception to this rule. Many serpent dragons and sea serpents were most likely sightings of giant snakes even larger than those we know today. Many species

become extinct every year, so it is very likely that giant snakes lived in the past and may still live today. One such account of a giant serpent dragon is the Carthiginian Serpent. In 250 B.C. Rome was engaged in a fierce conflict with Carthage over possession of Sicily. The Roman army, led by a man named Regulus, triumphantly approached the walls of Carthage, but when they reached the Bagrada River they were stopped by the appearance of a serpent dragon of enormous proportions. The army initially estimated that the dragon was some 100 feet long. The serpent made no aggressive moves towards the army, but it wouldn't let them pass, either. Regulus led his men further downstream to find another place to ford, but the dragon followed them, and it still would not let them pass.

Many men tried to confront the serpent head-on and many men died in the attempt. Regulus decided to attack the beast using the army's seige ballista, bombarding it with an avalanche of boulders. This tactic finally killed the beast, and when the soldiers measured, it was a whopping 120 feet long. The skin of the Carthiginian giant was taken to Capitol Hill and interred in one of the temples there, where it resided until about 133 B.C., after which it disappeared during a time of war.

The Dragon of Poseidon

When Perseus was returning from his task of slaying the Gorgon Medusa he chanced upon a young maiden staked out on a rock near the sea. Her name was Andromeda, the daughter of Cassiopeia. Not too long before, Cassiopeia had made the mistake of claiming that she was more beautiful than the Nerieds of the sea. In anger, Poseidon summoned the great sea serpent Cetus to wreak havoc on the coastal town.

An oracle told the monarchs that the slaughter and carnage would continue unless they offered Cetus their daughter Andromeda. Only then would Poseidon's anger be assuaged. Perseus waited for Cetus to arrive, determined to fight the dragon and win Andromeda's freedom. It was not long before Cetus appeared in all his terrible magnificence. Cetus was a huge sea serpent with a hound-like head sporting walrus tusks. A fiery red crest surrounded his head. Cetus lacked any true limbs, but retained vestigial fins along his torso.

Cetus ignored Perseus, focusing all his attention on Andromeda. In doing so, the dragon sealed its fate. Perseus, astride the great, winged Pegasus, swooped down and below the dragon's gaping jaws slipped his sword through a junction between the beast's scale plates, piercing its heart. Three times Perseus stabbed Cetus before the dragon fell, sinking beneath the waves and leaving Perseus to rescue Andromeda.

The Bride of the Lindorm King

In Klagonfort, Austria, you will find a fountain in a plaza that was inspired by the A.D. 1335, supposed discovery of a lindorm skull. The skull was later proven to be that of a wooly rhino, but the legends of the lindorms live on.

Long ago, shortly before the queen was due to give birth to twins, she went to consult a soothsayer. The soothsayer told her that upon returning to the palace she should eat two fresh onions. By doing so she was assured of having two healthy sons. The queen rushed away without hearing the rest of the soothsayer's advice. Upon her return to the palace the queen ate the first onion without peeling it first. Because the first one tasted so bad with the peeling on, she decided to peel the second onion before eating it.

Soon the time of birthing was upon the queen. The first child she gave birth to was male, but it was in no way human. It was a lindorm, a snake-like, wingless, two-legged dragon. Horrified that she could have given birth to such a thing, the queen bid the midwife to throw the lindorm prince out the window and into the woods. The second child came not long after and the younger of the two twins was a healthy, blond-haired, blue eyed boy.

Years passed, with both the lindorm prince and the boy prince growing up into full manhood (or dragonhood, whichever suits your fancy). It chanced to happen that while the prince was out searching for a bride he came upon his brother the lindorm. The lindorm confronted his younger brother, promising that he would not find a bride until his elder brother had obtained the true love of a willing bride. The prince brought many maidens before the lindorm, but none came willingly, so none were accepted.

Now, by lucky coincidence, before one young maiden was to go before the lindorm prince she happened to encounter the same soothsayer that the queen had visited so many years ago. The soothsayer gave the young maiden some advice on dealing with the lindorm. Armed with this advice, the girl went willingly to be the dragon's bride. She approached her new husband wearing a surprising number of dresses, which he ordered her to remove. She agreed to do so only if he would remove one layer of skin for every dress she took off. The lindorm, puzzled, agreed to her strange request. Finally, the maid was left with only a simple shift to cover her. She removed this last dress and stood before her husband completely naked. The lindorm then shed a final layer of skin, revealing not a lindorm but a handsome young man. This was the true visage of the elder prince. Because the queen had not peeled the first onion as the soothsayer would have warned her to, her first son was doomed to wear the dragon's skin until the maiden came along and freed him from his enchantment by peeling him as if he were an onion. The elder son and his wife were reinstated into the royal family and given the queen's blessings for a happy life.

The Wantly Dragon

In the time of Elizabeth I, in a small lodge called Wantly, there lived a fierce and terrible dragon with a penchant for trampling trees, eating up local livestock, and annoying the population. The people approached the master of Moore Hall, begging him to do something about the Wantly dragon. Moore agreed, under one condition. On the evening before the battle with the dragon, Moore was to be presented with a fair-skinned, dark-haired maiden to perform the duties of anointing his body and of dressing him the next morning. Moore then went to Sheffield, where he commissioned a custom suit of armor bristling with 6 inch spikes all over.

After all of the preparations had been made, Moore was ready to face the dragon. The custom armor was delivered. The young maiden was sent to anoint him and dress him in the morning. On the day Moore planned to confront the dragon, he went to a wellspring that the dragon was known to frequent. He climbed in and hid himself well, settling down to wait. When the dragon finally arrived, Moore leapt up and struck a blow to the jaw. Thus an epic battle that lasted two and a half days, during which neither Moore nor the Wantly dragon could gain the upper hand. Moore's spiked armor protected him, but the dragon's scales did likewise. Finally Moore latched onto the dragon's head, swung it around, and booted it in the rear, putting all of his might into the blow. The dragon yelped, leapt into the air, turned six times, and promptly died.

The Legend of Melusine

A long time ago, there was a lonely man by the name of Count of Anjou. He was sad because he was not married and had no one to care for him. Then, one day, much to everyone's surprise, Count Anjou returned from a trip with a lovely lady named Melusine. She was a beautiful lady with wonderful manners. Soon after their return, she and the Count were happily wed.

Melusine made a wonderful Countess. She was more than the people could have hoped for. She was noble, kind-hearted, and a great mother. Before too long though, people started to question the fact that the Count had married her. Nobody knew anything of her background, nor where she came from. But the greatest concern for the people was Melusine's terrible church attendance. She seldom attended Mass and when she did, she some-how always managed to disappear before the Eucharist was consecrated. This made the God-fearing locals very uncomfortable and nervous. What punishment might God bring about to the people of Anjou if their Countess wasn't a good Christian woman?

Upon hearing this, the Count became concerned. He ordered his guards to make sure that she stayed for the whole service next time. So at the next church service, Melusine tried to excuse herself before the Eucharist was prepared. The guards stopped her and as the priest finished the preparation of the Eucharist she screamed. It was an unearthly sound such as the people had never heard before. Melusine turned into a dragon and took flight, carrying two of her children away with her. Not all of Melusine's children went with her, some stayed and they later went on to become royalty.

The Legend of Melusine, Alternate Ending

In an alternate version Melusine was part of a large family. The father of this family was a terrible, cruel man. Melusine, as the eldest, decided to take it upon herself to get rid of the father. She tricked him into a cave and sealed him away, where he soon perished from lack of food. Unfortunately for Melusine, the Queen of the Fey Folk saw what she had done, and took offense. It was not for children to punish their parents, no matter how much the parents deserve it.

The Queen of the Faeries punished Melusine by making it so that each Saturday she would change into a half-dragon. Her lower body would change, becoming sleek-scaled with sharp clawed feet and a long, sinuous tail. The only way to keep the change from being permanent was to take a magickal bath each and every Saturday.

Time passed and Melusine was able to find a husband who agreed to be apart from her each Saturday and give her the privacy she requested. This worked out quite well for some time, until her husband gave in to curiosity. He wanted to see what his wife was up to each weekend. He peeked in on her during her bath one Saturday and saw her in her half-dragon form. With a shriek she turned into a full dragon and flew out the window, doomed to remain a dragon for the rest of her days.

The Legend of Saint Murrough and Paiste

In Ireland, shortly after the death of the beloved Saint Patrick, there came a great disturbance to the region around Lough Foyle. An ancient dragon by the name of Paiste was terrorizing the region. This dragon was huge, with ram's horns and potent venom. The people went to a holy man named Saint Murrough, for succor. The saint prayed to God for nine days and nine nights, then took three reed rods to where the dragon dwelt.

Paiste saw the saint coming and went out to meet him, telling him that he would be devoured. Saint Murrough remained calm and patient throughout the encounter. He agreed to let the dragon devour him if the dragon would indulge him in one simple experiment. Paiste agreed, thinking that none could harm him. Saint Murrough laid the three rods across the dragon's back and prayed as he had never prayed before. By the grace of God, the three rods grew over the great dragon, binding him in bonds stronger than steel.

Paiste struggled against the bonds. Enraged, he railed against Saint Murrough, claiming that he had been unfairly tricked. The saint made the dragon promise that he would no longer harm the Children of God. Paiste agreed, if only the saint would set him free. But Saint Murrough knew that the dragon's words were false and that he would not hold to his promise. Saint Murrough placed the dragon in the depths of Lough Foyle, where he is to be bound until the Day of Judgment should come to pass. Here Paiste patiently waits for the Day of Judgment, occasionally causing strange disturbances and odd tides and currents along the coasts of Lough Foyle.

The Gaoliang Bridge

Long ago in China, in what is now Bejing, the land was poor and marshy. A powerful dragon and his family ruled over the marshy land. The Ming Emperor wanted to build a great city. The God Nocha encouraged the Emperor to build his city on the dragon's lands.

The dragon watched angrily as the new city was built and in a fury he decided to seek revenge. The dragon figured that a city without water will fade away, so, determined to rid his lands of the invading humans, he decided to deprive the people of water. He disguised himself and his mate as an old man and old woman bearing water jugs. The dragon then appeared before the Emperor in a dream. During the dream the old man and old woman asked the Emperor's permission to take the water jugs out of the city. Unaware that the jugs contained all the water in the region, the Emperor bade them to take the jugs with his blessings. The next morning the Emperor was awoken by the cries of the people. All the water in the city and the surrounding area had dried up overnight, taken away by the dragon and his mate.

Now the God Nocha understood what had happened and he appeared to the chief builder of the city, Liu Bowen, with a way to get the water back. Liu was to find out who had left the city during the night. Asking at the city gates he was informed that an old man and an old woman carrying a hand cart had left the city during the night through the western gates. The road to the west led to the sea. Nocha told Liu that it was the dragons who had stolen the waters and that the jars had to be destroyed before they reached the sea or all of the waters of the region would be lost forever.

Only one soldier, Gaoliang, was brave enough to give chase after the dragons and attempt to stop them from stealing the waters. Liu gave Gaoliang a lance and bade him to catch up to the cart and pierce the jugs to release the waters. Liu warned Gaoliang that if he failed, the region would dry up, be in permanent drought, and the people would have to abandon the city. Gaoliang gave chase and soon caught up with the drag-ons. He managed to break one jar, but before he could pierce the second jar the waters pouring forth from the first swept him away from the cart. At this the dragons changed back into their true forms and Gaoliang had to flee back to the city with the task only half finished.

The roaring waters from the first jug followed Gaoliang all the way back to the city. When he reached the city he turned back to check on the water and drowned as the flood swept over him. The Gaoliang bridge was built to honor the brave warrior's noble deeds and stood for several centuries as a reminder of Gaoliang's sacrifice to bring the waters back to his people.

The Dragon Pearl

Long ago in China, a boy and his mother lived along the banks of the Min River. The family was poor, living day to day, unsure of where their next meal was coming from. The boy earned what he could by cutting grass and selling it to the villagers for their animals to eat. One summer there was no rain and the boy had to travel further and further away to find grass that was not dry and brown. Then one day he found a patch of fresh green grass and cut as much as he could carry. Day after day the young boy returned to harvest the patch, which strangly enough, stayed fresh and green. Soon, however, the boy grew tired of all the walking and cut a patch of turf to plant near his house.

Much to the boy's suprise and delight, when he pulled up the patch of turf he found a great pearl underneath. The boy pocketed the huge pearl and took home the patch of grass. He planted the grass by the side of the house and took the pearl to show his mother. The mother was delighted with her son's find and they stored the pearl in their near empty rice jar. The next day found the grass patch just as dry and brown as all the surrounding landscape. Mother and son decided to sell the pearl for money because their regular source of income had died. However, when they went to the rice jar they found it overflowing with rice. Assuming that the pearl was the cause of their great and magickal fortune, they put the pearl in their nearly empty money jar. The next day the money jar was full to the brim with coins. The small family had enough money and rice to keep them well for quite some time.

Though the pair told no one about the pearl, it swiftly became obvious that the family had come into some money. One day robbers broke into the house to try and steal some of the wealth they thought was hidden there. In a panic the young boy swallowed the pearl so that the thieves would not get their hands on it. No sooner than he swallowed it than his insides started to roil and burn, as if he had swallowed acid instead of a cool, hard pearl.

The boy raced out of the house and to the well where he guzzled water, trying vainly to quench the fierce fire burning in his gut. The well water did not help, so the boy ran to the river to drink. As he reached the bank, the boy changed. His body grew longer and larger and scales sprouted along its length. His face elongated into a whiskered muzzle, horns sprouted from his head, and wings from his back. The pearl had changed him into a dragon! As the newly created dragon dove into the river that was to be his new home, the heavens opened up and poured forth rains to heal the parched earth and end the drought.

The Legend of Pai Lung

One night an old man was caught in a fierce storm. He stopped at a house to beg for shelter for the night. A young girl answered the door and allowed him to come in. The girl's parents let the old man stay with them overnight so that he would not have to be out in the gale. He was gone by the time the family had risen in the morning. However, the girl was soon discovered to be pregnant. Her family became enraged and threw her out of the house, mortified by her apparent indiscretion.

The girl made her lonely way in the world and in due time the baby was born. This baby though, was no normal child. When he was born he was nothing more than a ball of white fur. The horrified mother threw the fur ball into the sea, whereupon it turned into a magnificent white dragon. The girl was terrified and died from fright.

Her tainted reputation was repaired, for obviously the girl had been dragon blessed. People revered her memory as she was the mother of the great Pai Lung, the white dragon. The girl was given a decent burial and a temple was erected over the site. People would go to the temple to leave offerings and to ask for favors from Pai Lung. A tablet with the Legend of Pai Lung was placed at the site of the temple.

Golden Dragon Yu

The Yellow Emperor, supreme God of the Chinese, looked down over the Earth and was dismayed by how evil and wicked humans had become. The Yellow Emperor ordered the rain god to make the rains flow endlessly and rid the Earth of humanity's wickedness. The resulting flood starting killing off all of the plants, animals, and people. The Yellow Emperor's grandson, Kun, pleaded with his grandfather to end the rains, but the Yellow Emperor refused the request.

Kun then met an old tortoise who told him that to end the rains he needed some magick mud, and that the Yellow Emperor kept a jar of it in his treasury. Kun went to his grandfather's palace, into the treasury, and stole the jar of magick mud. With the jar in hand, Kun started spreading the magick mud around. Wherever the mud touched, islands formed, and the waters dried up. Kun spread it all over, making new land.

Unfortunately the Yellow Emperor saw what Kun was doing and he sent the fire god down to kill him. Kun saw the fire god approaching and transformed into a white horse, fleeing to find a hiding spot. The fire god chased Kun and finally managed to strike him down. Kun's body was left where it lay, and as time passed a new life grew within the old shell of the body. This was Yu, son of Kun. Yu was a beautiful dragon with golden scales, a magnificent mane, and five claws per paw.

Yu went to see the Yellow Emperor, hoping to finish what Kun had started. He begged his great-grandfather to end the floodwaters. The Yellow Emperor finally relented, granting Yu the title of rain god and giving him enough magick mud to restore the lands. The great golden dragon ended the rains and, with the help of the old tortoise, used the magick mud to build the lands back up.

Yu then used his massive tail to plow rivers through the lands and channel the waters to the seas. While carving out the Yellow River he ran into some problems in the form of some tough, rocky cliffs. This area he named Dragon's Gate, and it became a place sacred to both dragons and humans. It was here that fish could attempt the trial of the Gate and so turn into dragons. When the people saw what Yu had done for them, they pleaded with him to be their Emperor. Yu assented to the people's request. He changed his form, becoming human and ruling China as Emperor. This is why the Imperial Dragon is a five-toed dragon and why the Chinese call themselves the "People of the Dragon" or the "Children of the Dragon."

The Koshi Dragon

One day, while walking along the banks of the river Hinokami, the warrior Susawono came across an elderly couple and a young lady, all of whom were crying. Susawono asked the group why they were so sad. The elderly couple told Susawono that the young girl was the last of their eight daughters. Every year for the last seven, a dragon who lived along the Koshi had come and abducted one of the daughters and devoured her. The time during which the dragon attacked the family was fast approaching and the family was scared that they were to lose their remaining daughter.

In exchange for the young maiden's hand in marriage, Susawono agreed to face the Koshi dragon and slay him. The couple told Susawono that the dragon was immense, sporting eight heads with flaming eyes, and eight whip-like tails. This description did nothing to deter Susawono, and he set out to make his preparations. First Susawono used magick to turn his bride into a comb which he hid in his hair to keep safe from the dragon. He then gave the parents a recipe for some very potent sake and instructed them to brew as much of it as they could. Once that was done he acquired eight large vats which he placed along the road. Susawono and the girl's parents then filled each of the eight vats with the powerful, steaming alcoholic beverage.

The aroma of the alcohol enticed the Koshi dragon and it came to investigate. The dragon stuck each of its eight muzzles into the huge sake vats and guzzled it all down, whereupon it became very drunk. Susawono then appeared to do battle with the drunken, staggering dragon. The battle was short and rather one-sided, and in no time at all Susawono slew the Koshi Dragon. After the dragon was slain, he turned the young maiden back into her natural form and her family rejoiced. The family kept their promise to the valiant, cunning warrior and the pair were wed that same day and lived happily for the rest of their lives.

Kiyo's Lesson

Once there was a young lady named Kiyo who worked at a restaurant in her town. A priest from a nearby temple saw her going to and from work. This priest fell in love with Kiyo and eventually broke the temple rules by entering the tea house and speaking with her. In doing so he lost all sense of his religious obligations and started going out with the beautiful young waitress. For a while, things were good and both enjoyed one another's company. But soon enough the priest grew bored with her. He left Kiyo and returned to the temple.

Needless to say, this enraged Kiyo. The young lady went away and studied magick at a distant temple. Through her diligent studies, Kiyo learned the secret to turn from human to dragon and back again. Having mastered this rare skill, Kiyo went back home and attacked her former lover's temple. The priest grew quite scared and tried to hide in the bell at the top of the temple, but it was no use. Kiyo burned the belltower and melted the bell, killing the priest in the process. Thus, Kiyo had her revenge.

The Legend of Yofune-Nushi

Yofune-Nushi lived in a cave located under Oki Island. Now Yofune-Nushi, unlike most other Asian dragons, was a mean, vicious dragon who forced the people of the local village to make a virgin sacrifice every year on June 13th. He threatened to create a massive storm to destroy the village's fishing fleet if they disobeyed him. As fishing was the only way the village earned their income, they found that they could not refuse.

One year, on June 13th, a maid of Tokyo came forward to offer herself as Yofune-Nushi's sacrifice. The villagers willingly took her to the sacrificial island and left her to wait for the dragon. When Yofune-Nushi appeared, the girl did not cringe or cower before him. Rather, she pulled out a knife she had hidden within the folds of her kimono and slashed at the great beast's eyes. Roaring in pain, the dragon reared up, exposing his vulnerable underbelly to the girl, whereupon she seized her chance and slew him.

Marduk and Tiamat

According to Assyrin-Babylonian myth, the two primordial beings at the beginning of the world were Tiamat and Apsu. From these two sprang a great and varied dynasty of gods and goddesses. These gods lived in peace with their ancestors, but as time went on they eventually started challenging the Ancient ones. Incensed, Apsu and a rather reluctant Tiamat plotted their progeny's destruction.

Somehow the gods and goddesses found out their parents' plan and they got the jump on Apsu, slaying him before he could do anything. Upon hearing this, Tiamat forgot the erstwhile love she had felt for her children and began plotting against them in earnest. Potent hatred fueled her actions and thoughts and she created a monstrous army to send against the gods. In this mighty army were men with the tails of fish and men with tails like scorpion stings. There were great serpent-wurms, hounds with eyes of fire, and living storms.

Tiamat, in the form of a fierce dragon with dagger-like talons and curved horns on her head, led the monstrous army. The gods were appalled, but after much thought Marduk, the Sun god, agreed to fight Tiamat and her horde of creatures on one condition: If he was successful, then they must name him the supreme god over all. The others, desperate to have a champion against the enraged Tiamat, agreed to Marduk's terms. Marduk set about his tasks with a huge net, a bow and quiver of arrows and (most importantly), the allegiance of the hurricane.

Marduk set himself against the great Tiamat and after much struggle, bound her tightly in the net. He sent a hurricane to assail her, and when she opened her mouth to devour the sentient storm, Marduk fired arrows into her unprotected, vulnerable belly. He continued with his assault until Tiamat was no more. Marduk then cut the great primordial dragon's body in half, using one half to create the heavens and the other to create the earth.

The Pearl of Kinabalu

At the top of Mount Kinabalu in Borneo, a dragon named Kinabalu lived. He was the keeper of a wondrous Pearl of Wisdom, greater than most other dragons' pearls. This pearl was so wondrous that the Emperor of China grew covetous and sought to obtain it, for dragon jewels are great sources of power. The Emperor sent many warriors to retrieve it, but all were vanquished by Kinabalu. Finally, the Emperor sent Wee Ping and Wee San, two of his best warriors, to gain possession of the Pearl.

Wee San devised a plan to get the pearl from Kinabalu. He decided to wait until the dragon had left to feed and then he and Wee San would use a kite to rise to the top of the mountain. Once there, they would snag the pearl, replace it with an imitation, and flee to safety. They succeeded in taking the pearl and replacing it with the fake. However, when Kinabalu returned he immediately recognized the deception and chased after the two. By the time the dragon caught up with the warriors they were at sea. Wee San ordered that the cannon be fired at the angry dragon. Kinabalu, thinking that the cannon ball was his stolen pearl, swallowed it up and thus perished.

When they returned home, Wee Ping, feeling left out of everything, said that he was the one who had devised the plan to steal the pearl, rather than Wee San. He also said that he was the one who ordered the cannon to be fired, thus resulting in the death of the dragon. Wee San, wanting no conflicts, left China and went on to become the leader of the Brunei. Wee Ping, however, fell into great ruin because of his lies.

Indra and Vritra

Long ago, before the world was fully formed, Indra was the god of all warriors. He was also a god of nature and a bringer of the rains. Now Indra had no enemies save one—Vritra, a great, limbless dragon who held in his belly all the waters of the heavens.

Vritra refused to release the waters of the heavens so that Indra could nourish the earth. After many such refusals to return the heavenly waters, Indra decided that the only way to get the waters back was to slay Vritra. Otherwise everything on earth would perish for lack of rain.

Indra, using the Sun as his chariot and lightning bolts as his arrows, went to meet Vritra in battle. As the battle went on, Indra seemed to be losing. Vritra wound about him, trapping him in suffocating coils. Vritra, sure of victory, made the mistake of taking his eyes off of his captive. That was all Indra needed. The warrior god quickly made his move and released a thunderbolt arrow that slew the mighty dragon. Vritra fell down a mountainside, his great body bursting open to release all of the heavenly waters. These waters formed the seas we know today. Indra's Sun chariot rose into the sky, and so the first dawn broke upon a new world.

Endings

This is the legend of Dun'marra, which I have rewritten as a poem.

The time of ending has come.
The Seven awaken from their age old slumber.
Their memory has been lost to humankind;
set loose on the eddies of time.
But man shall know their fury again.
The One calls to them,
setting them loose to recreate the world.

First to awaken is Grael the Black,
she who is called Lady Wardragon.
Black scales glitter in the dark light,
red eyes flare bright.
The great creature tilts her head and roars,
a deep, reverberating sound.
She calls to the others and one by one they too come alive.
Ayahz the White, Master Healer.
Bahamut, Lord of Time.
Freyeth, Keeper of the Flames.
Gaia, Mother Earth Dragon.
Rai, Thunder Lord.
Tiama'at, Mistress of all Waters.

Humankind has forgotten the teachings of the One.
So, too, have they forgotten the might of the Divine Dragons,
the Seven Patrons of the Elements.
Too late they remember, far too late to make amends.

Grael's fury washes over the world.
She is the primal force of Chaos; her fires scouring the land clean.
Rai follows, calling the storms together.
Wind and rain tear down the follies of men.
From deep within, the earth trembles.
World around Freyeth releases the devastation of the earth's inner fires,
lava covers cities and fields alike, ash hiding the sun's rays.

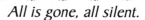
All is gone, all silent.
Behind the holocaust wrought by the dragons of chaos come the healers.
Ayahz's breath clears the land of debris.
Gaia reshapes the land,
creating new fields and forests.
Tiama'at fills the lakes, streams, rivers, and oceans of the new world.
Bahamut is last.
The Lord of Time is of both chaos and order.
Second to only the Master Healer and the Lady Wardragon,
it is he who shall initiate the new world into full life.
The silvery dragon closes his eyes,
singing the words of the Making.
He calls into being those who will inhabit the world next,
all the animals, plants, and other beings,
who will take the place of all those long gone.

Satisfied with the work of the Patron Dragons,
the One sends them back to sleep, one by one,
not to awaken again until they are needed.
So this cycle shall continue for time immemorial,
until chaos and order reach complete harmony within themselves.

The Uktena and the Tlanuhwa

When the world was young all living things were great in size. Among these were the Uktena and the Tlanuhwa. The Uktena were beautiful serpents of enormous size, with shiny, iridescent scales, giant buzzard-wings, and horns upon their heads like great stags. The Uktena sported a gem called an ulunsuti upon their foreheads. This gem is one of the most lucky and powerful objects that a man can own. The ulunsuti contains great medicine. These stones must be kept in a circular buckskin pouch, along with a bit of red pigment. It must also be kept in a dry, safe place away from people. It was believed that the Uktena could travel between this world and the underworld through the network of caves found under the rivers and lakes.

The Tlanuhwa were hawks of gigantic size. These birds were marked as the red-tail hawks of today, thus they are believed to be the original progenitors of these beautiful birds. Along the Tennessee River one can find the ancient cave homes of the Tlanuhwa. Near the caves was a human settlement. For the longest time the people had no problem with the giant birds dwelling nearby. But one day the Tlanuhwa started swooping down and plucking children from the village. Needless to say, the villagers pan-icked, the women demanding that the men do something to protect the children and the village.

The men of the village gathered together and came up with a plan to combat the Tlanuhwa. Using sturdy vines the men made long ropes with which to climb down from the top of the cliffs to the Tlanuhwa caves. They waited until all the birds had gone hunting to carry out their plan. The men climbed down the vine ropes and what do you think they found? All the village children safe and sound. The Tlanuhwa had a nest full of eggs in the cave and they had stolen the children as food for the chicks after they hatched. The men got all of the children out of the cave safely, but soon the Tlanuhwa returned bearing freshly caught children. The men started chucking the giant bird eggs out of the caves and into the river below. The great Uktena who lived in the river surfaced and began eating the eggs.

This action so enraged the Tlanuhwa that they dropped the children they were carrying and dived at the Uktena. The men were lucky enough to catch the falling children and they took all of them back to the village while the giant beasts fought. Eventually the Tlanuhwa prevailed and scattered the pieces of the Uktena across the land. After the battle, the Tlanuhwa flew up into the clouds and disappeared, never to be seen again by humans.

Legends

The Devil's Hole

The Devil's Hole, a giant fissure in Boone County, Arkansas, was believed to have been the home of a gowrow at one time. The fissure was on the property of E. J. Rhodes. One day Rhodes got it in his head to explore the fissure and see if it held anything of interest. He reached a depth of 200 feet before being halted at a rock ledge. After this point it was too narrow a shaft for a human with gear to descend.

With the help of a few friends, Rhodes first lowered a rope with an iron rod attached and then two or three ropes with big rocks attached after that. After a few intrusions into the shaft, a fierce hissing, like one coming from an angry animal was heard. The iron rod was bent when they pulled it back up and the ropes with the rocks attached had been neatly bitten in two. No animal was ever coaxed out of the fissure, but by common consent it was believed to be a gowrow.

The Sea Serpent of Spoonville Beach

The people of Spoonville Beach were going through a time of bad luck. It just so happened that some of the fishermen had gone out to fish for awhile. During their trip they happened to spot something unusual—a sea serpent! The fishermen sped back to shore and told of their encounter. The story spread like wildfire and soon enough it was reported in the papers. The story attracted tourists who flocked to the beaches in hopes of spotting the sea serpent for themselves. Now business was good for the small town, but soon enough it dwindled away, as no one spotted the beast again.

When business had tapered off once more, a few people set out in a boat and came back with yet more stories of the sea serpent. They described it as being covered in green scales and having glowing red eyes. Smoke billowed out of its mouth and nose. People once again flocked to the shore in hopes of getting a quick glimpse of the beast. Two people went out in a boat and had a close up enounter with the beast. Of the two, one was terrified and never wanted to try again. The other however, wanted to try his luck once more. He set out again to see the beast despite the pleadings of his friend to stay ashore. No one knows whether or not he found the beast. Neither the man nor his boat were ever seen again.

Gloucester's Sea Serpent

In August of 1817, numerous sea serpent sightings in Boston Harbor were reported. This was not just an isolated phenomenon as many people saw the black-scaled creature. It was reported to be some 40 to 55 feet in length and had a head greatly resembling that of a horse. In all accounts, the sea serpent moved with the vertical undulations more common to caterpillars rather than with the horizontal undulations common to serpents.

The government finally decided to get involved and the Linnaean Society of New England put together a team to investigate. Members of the Linnaean team included Judge John Davis, Dr. Jakob Bigelow, and the naturalist Francis Gray. A short time later a black, serpentine creature washed up on the harbor's shores. The team did an autopsy on it, but found it to be nothing more than a severely deformed black snake. Sightings of the beast tapered off and finally ceased.

The Seven Headed Dragon: An Ojibwa Legend

A long time ago a man and his wife lived with their horse and dog along the banks of a lake. Their diet consisted mostly of fish caught in the lake, but as it sometimes happens with such things, the pair went through a time when no fish were caught. They grew very hungry. Finally, one day when the man went to check his nets, he found a fish trapped inside.

Elated, he pulled the fish up and prepared to kill it. However, this was no ordinary fish, and before he could strike it the fish spoke. It told the man not to kill it right away. Instead the man was to take all of the scales off and bury them in the garden. Along with the scales, the man was to cut the fish's fins off and bury them in the garden as well. He was to cut off the head and feed it to his wife, give half the body to the dog and the other half to the horse. After all this was done, the fish instructed the man to shut up the stable and not open it for four days and four nights, no matter what.

The man took the fish home and followed all of the instructions, hoping and praying for good luck to follow. After the wife had eaten the fish she became pregnant, and on the fourth day she gave birth to twins. Elated, the man ran to the barn and checked the horse. Miraculously the mare had

Seven Headed Hydra

given birth to twin foals, and the dog to twin pups during the same time. Fortune followed fortune. The man and wife went to the garden and dug up the scales and fins. The scales had become silver money and the fins sharp swords.

The family began catching many fish. Time passed and the boys grew up. One day the brothers were talking and the eldest began wondering if there were any other people in the world. The younger insisted that there must be, so the elder brother decided to set out to find the truth. The elder brother packed his belongings and set out with his horse and faithful dog.

After a long day's travel, the elder brother came to a spring with silvery waters. He decided to stop here and rest. Setting up camp, he went to the spring to get some water. But when his hands brushed against the surface his pinky finger turned into silver. The elder brother was amazed. He then put some water on his dog's ears, his horse's ears, and in his hair, all of which turned to silver shortly thereafter.

When at last the elder brother came to a large human settlement, he took off his garments and clad himself in rags. He tied a kerchief over his head and a bandage around his silver finger. Next he charmed his dog and horse to make them small and tucked them into a box. He approached a blacksmith's shop and found food and lodging in exchange for doing chores around the smithy. The elder brother spent many long months in the blacksmith's company. One day the blacksmith came back home looking very sad. When the brother asked what was wrong, the blacksmith told him that it was time for the offering to the Manitou, a fearsome seven-headed dragon. This time, the village chief's daughter had been chosen to be the sacrifice; she was to be staked out the next day.

The next morning the brother left the village, put his own clothes back on, and returned his dog and horse to normal size. They set out along the path, and sure enough they soon came upon a pretty, young maiden staked to a pole and crying pitifully. He approached her and asked what she was doing. At first she refused to speak with him, but finally he coaxed the story out of her. She had been left for the dragon to eat. If a sacrifice was not offered each year, the terrible manitou would terrorize the countryside and slaughter all it came across. The elder brother untied her and bade her stay there. He would go ahead and slay the dragon. She gave him a special ring and said that she would wait for his return, though she did express doubts about his ability to kill the dragon.

The elder brother rode further down the road and finally came to the Manitou's lair. The very trees shook with the dragon's breathing, but this did not deter him at all. Man, horse, and dog engaged the dragon in a battle that lasted for days. Finally they succeeded in cutting off all of the dragon's seven heads. With the beast dead, the brother cut out the tongues from each of the heads and wrapped them up. He returned to the girl and showed her the evidence of the dead dragon. He bade her to take the tongues to her father and tell him that the dragon had been slain by a young man, but that she did not know who he was.

The girl began her journey home and met the blacksmith that the elder brother had stayed with. He was shocked that she had come back, and was fearful that the dragon would destroy the village. She insisted that the manitou was dead and finally showed him the dragon's tongues as proof. When he asked who killed it, she told him that a young man had, but that she didn't know who he was. The blacksmith decided to take advantage of the situation. He threatened to kill the young girl if she did not tell her father that *he* was the one who had slain the beast. Fearfully, she agreed. The blacksmith accompanied her back to her parent's house and told of the dragon's defeat. The chief was overjoyed. He agreed to marry his daughter to the blacksmith in four day's time. Meanwhile, the elder brother had returned secretly to the village, donned his rags, and shrunk his horse and dog. He got back just in time to hear the announcement of the celebrations leading up to the wedding.

On the fourth day the elder brother put on his proper clothes and tied the ring about his neck. He went to sit before the chief's house. When the girl came outside she recognized him immediately. Secretly she went and told her father the truth of the matter and pointed out the real dragon slayer to him. Outraged, the Chief put the blacksmith to death for his lies and then married his daughter to the elder brother. In addition, he gave him property and money, as thanks for saving his daughter.

The Legend of Coatlcue

Coatlcue was once the priestess of a shrine high up in the mountains. One day, while she was cleaning the shrine, a ball of feathers descended from the sky and landed upon her breast. Coatlcue gave little thought to the feathers. Rather absentmindedly she tucked the ball of feathers into her belt. When she later looked for the feathers, they were nowhere to be found. Several days later Coatlcue found herself pregnant and attributed it to the feathers.

Coatlcue already had some children, one of them being the Moon goddess Coyolxauhqui. When her many children discovered that she was pregnant, they became jealous and suspicious of her claim that the pregnancy was a miracle. The children gathered at the foot of the mountain housing the shrine. The Moon goddess urged her brothers to punish Coatlcue for promiscuity. They decided to put their mother to death. From her mountain shrine Coatlcue heard her children and their plotting. She quailed in fear, but then heard a voice from her womb. It told her not to be afraid, that everything would be alright. Her new child would protect her.

When Coyolxauhqui and her brothers stormed up the mountain to the shrine, Huitzilopochtli emerged to face them. Fully grown, his skin was painted blue and he wore body armor in a style that would later become adopted by all Aztec warriors. Huitzilopochtli's left leg was sheathed in hummingbird feathers, the same type of feathers that had fallen upon Coatlcue's breast. With a xiuhcoatl, Huitzilopochtli slew his sister and most of his brothers, allowing only a few to escape his wrath.

Quetzalcoatl and Tezcatlipoca Join Forces

Under most circumstances Quetzalcoatl and Tezcatlipoca were the worst of enemies. But one day a huge Earth Monster named Tlaltecuhtli began wandering the land. This fearsome beast had a gaping mouth with huge fangs, and also sported mouths at her knees and elbows. In order to defeat Tlaltecuhtli, Quetzalcoatl and Tezcatlipoca decided to join forces. They appeared in the form of great serpents. The pair fought and fought with the great Earth Monster and finally they managed to tear the beast in half. One piece they hurled into the air to make the sky. The remaining piece they laid out flat, and thus created the Earth.

The other gods were less than pleased by the death of the Earth Monster. They declared that although she was dead, the "earth" part of her body would provide for future life. They made trees and herbs from her hair and grass and sweet flowers grew from her skin. The life-giving waters of wells and springs came from her eyes. Her mouth made rivers and large, subterranean caverns, and her nose became the mountain peaks and deep valleys of the Sierras. Thus did the feuding gods help to create the Earth.

The Legend of Bida

Long ago, in the city of Wagadu, it would rain gold three times a year. Why would it do this, you might ask? The grandfather of the current town chief, Lagarre, had made a pact with the dragon Bida. Each year the dragon would be given 10 maidens as an offering. For this payment, Bida would reward the village with showers of gold three times a year.

Now Lagarre, with the aid of wise Koliko, negotiated a different payment with Bida. Lagarre was tired of sacrificing so many people to the dragon.

Under the new terms, the dragon would get just one maiden a year for the gold. Amazingly, Bida agreed, and for three years this worked out fine. Then the day came for Sia Jatta Bari, perhaps the most beautiful maiden in all of Wagadu, to be sacrificed. Sia was dressed in marriage attire and taken to the dragon's home, to be consumed by the fierce beast. However, Sia's lover, Mamadi Sefe Dekote, did not wish her to die, so he rode out with the sacrificial procession.

Mamadi had a plan for defeating the dragon. It was Bida's habit to stick his head and neck out of his cave three times, and on the last time he would snatch up his victim. Mamadi maneuvered to be close to Sia and on the third time that Bida stuck his head out, Mamadi struck him down. Unfortunately for Mamadi and the townspeople, the blow was not clean. With his dying breath the great wurm cursed the town. The golden rain would not fall for seven years, seven weeks, and seven days. Enraged, the townspeople chased Mamadi and Sia from Wagadu. Luckily for the pair, Mamadi's uncle helped them and gave them a safe place to stay.

But this story does not have a happy ending. Not only did the golden rain stop, but Sia did not really love Mamadi. Despite all his sacrifices for her, she deceived him. Sia tricked Mamadi into cutting off a finger and a toe, then told him that she could never love someone who only had nine toes and nine fingers. She could only love one who had 10 fingers and 10 toes. Angered and hurt, Mamadi turned to a Witch who gave him a potion that made Sia instantly fall in love with him. Afterward Mamadi tricked Sia into sleeping with his servant, whereupon she died of pure shame. The story of Bida is a warning against being greedy.

Hotu-puku

Many years ago, travelers going between Rotorua and Taupo began disappearing. Thinking that neighboring people were the problem, a war band set out to end the problem. Instead of finding raiders though, the war band found a taniwha, whom they called Hotu-puku. The warriors tried attacking the massive dragon, but all they succeeded in doing was anger-ing the beast. Hotu-puku attacked, killing almost the entire war band. The rest fled for their lives so as they could tell the tale of the dragon to their people.

A man named Pitaka organized a dragon-hunting party and put a plan together. Using himself as bait, the crafty hunter snuck a noose around the beast's tail. Using the first snare to keep Hotu-puku from getting away, the hunters managed to snag another one around it's neck. The dragon began thrashing about and eventually strangled itself with the noose. After the beast was dead it was cut open to make sure that it was the same one that had killed the war band. Sure enough, they found the remains in the dragon's belly. They buried the victims, and roasted and dined upon the dragon for dinner.

Kataore

Pitaka had more encounters with the taniwha dragons. In the same region near Rotorua, the dragon Kataore began causing trouble. Kataore was the pet of a local chief, named Tangaroa-mihi. Kataore was not tame however, and the taniwha soon started attacking people. He took up resi-dence in a nearby cave and began eating travelers. One of Kataore's last victims was Tuhikarapapa, a high-born lady.

Tuhikarapapa was engaged to a man named Reretoi, and he was more than upset at the death of his betrothed. Reretoi put together a party to slay the marauding dragon, even going so far as to call upon the tohunga, or local wizards, to use magick to drain the beast's strength. Pitaka joined Reretoi's group and put together a plan for facing the land-dwelling taniwha. As he did with Hotu-puku, Pitaka used stealth and cunning to enter the dragon's cave and slip a series of nooses around it's neck. Once firmly in place, the men outside pulled them taut, dragging the taniwha out of the cave. The dragon's own thrashing caused it to strangle itself. As with Hotu-puku, the dragon was roasted and a feast was had.

Chapter 3

Dragons in the Modern Realm

Dragons have flown in the imaginations of humanity for ages untold. Today, perhaps, they are even more popular than ever before. Dragons soar on the big screen, stampede through literature, and wing their way through the gaming worlds. We have already covered the dragons and dragon myths of the world, now we will explore dragons in the modern realms of film, literature, and gaming.

Dragons in the Realm of Gaming

Dragons have long been a staple of traditional RPGs. Perhaps the best known is the popular *Dungeons and Dragons*. Then, of course, there are the *D&D* spinoffs such as *Dragonlance* and *Forgotten Realms*, each with a different set of attendent dragons.

Not only are dragons featured prominently in traditional RPGs, but as the computer age has made video games more and more accessible, they have made a home for themselves in video game RPGs. Some well-known

RPGs that include dragons are the *Final Fantasy* series, the *Breath of Fire* series, *Lunar: Silver Star Story Complete*, and *Pokemon*, among many others.

Dungeons and Dragons

Dungeons and Dragons (*D&D*)has gone through three revisions, if not more, since its creation in the 1970s. The dragons of *Dungeons and Dragons* are immense creatures of all shapes and sizes. For the most part, these dragons resemble the classical European dragon, with four feet and bat-like wings, though as we shall see, that is not always the case. These dragons can live for thousands of years and only grow more powerful and wise as time passes. They tend to be egotistical and are susceptible to flattery. Most of them can speak more than one language; often they speak three or four fluently. All dragon species have excellent senses compared to humans, and some older dragons even gain the ability to see invisible beings.

The dragons of *D&D* fall into two different categories: Lawful and Chaotic. Within each order a dragon may be good, evil, or neutral. All of the Chaotic dragons are chromatic in color: green, blue, red, and black. All of the Lawful dragons are metallic in color: bronze, silver, gold, and brass.

Black Dragons: These are the most evil-tempered of all the *D&D* dragons. They prefer to make their homes in bogs, swamps, and other such stagnant places. They may also choose to dwell in dense tropical rain forests or jungles. While they have no natural enemies, they will attack anything unlucky enough to cross paths with them. Black dragons prefer submerged cavern lairs with both an underwater and a land exit/entrance. These dragons are identified by their deep-set eye sockets and giant horns protruding from their cheeks. Smaller horns and spikes grace its head. When the mouth is closed most of the teeth protrude, as a crocodile's teeth. In addition, it is not uncommon for this dragon to drool a highly acidic saliva. A black dragon's diet consists mostly of mollusk, fish, and other aquatic creatures, though it will hunt red meat on occasion. Like most dragons, these are especially fond of hoarding and love coins.

They will capture humanoid creatures and quiz them on coin stashes that they might be able to get to before killing their helpless victims. These dragons utilize acid to attack.

Blue Dragons: These dragons are vain, territorial beasts. They favor the hot, arid desert-like places. Blues are fierce fighters and look on cowards with scorn. Most of all they detest brass dragons, with their propensity to flee from battles. Blue dragons prefer underground burrows and will not bother to clear sand out from the burrow entrance. They simply tunnel through the sand. This serves as an effective means to hide the entrance. These dragons are identified by their oversized frilled ears and the great horn jutting from their forehead. When burrowing, a blue's ears can furl closed to keep sand from getting in. The nostrils are set close to the eyes in the blunt-muzzled head.

Small horny bumps run from the nostrils up along the brow ridge. Underneath a blue dragon's chin is a bristling beard of horns. As with the black dragons, a blue's teeth protrude even when the mouth is closed. And similar to black dragons, blues treasure gems above all else in its hoard. These dragons use a lightning breath attack.

Red Dragons: Reds are very covetous dragons, and are constantly seeking to enlarge their treasure hoards. Reds prefer mountains or badlands for their homes, with plenty of places to perch high and survey their lands. Volcanic cave lairs are ideal for these dragons. Reds have two massive, backswept horns on the top of their heads, and large cheek frills with spikes. The large ears often merge with the cheek frills as the dragon matures. They have chin and nose spikes with smaller horns that run both above and below the eye orbits. A long crest runs from the top of the head down along the back. These dragons are the archetypal "evil" fire-breathing dragon. Reds are exceedingly vengeful, ferocious, and avaricious. These dragons have the largest hoards of any of the dragon species, and they know the exact amount of treasure and its value. A red will notice if even a single coin is missing and will become enraged at even a minor theft. Reds prefer meat above all else, and value human or elfin youth as delicacies.

Green Dragons: Greens are masters of intrigue and subterfuge. They tend to be very belligerent, territorial, and aggressive. Green dragons will attack with the least provocation. They prefer to live in old forests. They will make lairs in caves, on sheer cliffs, or in hillsides. Greens specialize in using magick on vegetation and will cover lair entrances with magically grown plants. Green dragons have crocodilian heads set on a long neck. They have small, stubby brow spikes and a massive frill that runs down their backs. Greens will eat anything, even resorting to the edible plant matter when hungry enough. A green's favorite food? Elves! Green dragons collect anything for their hoards; they aren't too picky. Greens use chlorine breath as their weapon.

White Dragons: White dragons are the smallest and least intelligent of the dragon species. They are the epitome of the single-minded hunter. These dragons have sleek heads with beak-like mouths. They have small chin and throat spikes and a small, horny bump on the forehead. A crest, akin to a shark's dorsal fin, decorates the head as well. They have ear openings in the sides of their heads much as lizards do, and thick armor-plate scales along the neck. These dragons live in the frigid arctic climates and prefer food that has been frozen. White dragons enjoy treasures that reflect the beauty of ice and snow such as diamonds. These dragons use an ice breath weapon.

Gold Dragons: These dragons have a very strong sense of justice, and will pursue and root out evil no matter what the cost. Golds are happy to live just about anywhere, so long as they can have a spacious lair made of stone with numerous rooms. A gold dragon usually has lair guards comprised of local animals, storm giants, or cloud giants. These dragons have a pair of backturned horns on their heads and two smaller sets of horns that have a smooth, polished metallic look to them. These horns run along the cheeks. On each side of their chins they have a short frill. Numerous catfish barbels grace the muzzle and a large frill runs down the back along the spine. Golds will often maintain an assumed state, usually in the form of some kind of domestic animal such as a dog or cat. Gold dragons are very patient and considerate, making them very good listeners and advice givers. They prefer parley to fighting, but are fearsome foes when aroused. In hoard building, golds prefer the more artistic treasures like paintings, sculpture, and porcelain.

Silver/Platinum Dragons: Silvers enjoy the company of humans and will often take the form of elderly males to mingle with them. Though they loathe injustice and cruelty, silvers are not as apt to actively hunt wrong-doers. They are more concerned with protecting the innocent and healing those who are injured. These dragons prefer mountainous homes along with the reds. They particularly prefer high mountains, so that they may be near the vast, open skies. They love to fly and will do so for hours— simply for the pleasure of it. Silvers may have lairs in the clouds themselves, enchanted places with solid, stable bottoms. Silvers have two great, back-swept horns on their heads and giant cheek/ear frills as the reds do, but they are not spiky. They have a chin frill rather than chin spikes and a huge frill running from the forehead down along the back all the way to the tail tip that gives this dragon species the appearance of having a mohawk! Silvers are omnivorous and will live off of humans fare just fine. For treasures, these dragons prefer things of exquisite workmanship. A silver dragon prefers not to fight unless faced with an evil or patently aggressive foe. In battle they will attempt to stay in their assumed forms and use magick to end the battle before it gets too out of hand.

Brass Dragons: The dragons are fun-loving and gregarious. They love hot, arid areas just as the blues do and this usually puts them at odds with their much more aggressive and more powerful cousins. Brass dragons will put their superior speed to work and out fly an attacking blue. A Brass' most distinguishable feature is the fluted crest on the back of its head. Because brasses are burrowers just like blues, the crest is used like a plow, helping them in tunneling. These dragons have two sharp horns protruding from the underside of their chins. Brass dragon wings are short affairs that run from the shoulders to past the tail tip. These wings are supported by stiff spines running perpendicular to the backbone. Brass dragons need little in the way of sustenance. They can survive on very little food and drink the dew that collects in the morning time. Brass dragons prefer organic treasures over other things. They value items made of rare woods, textiles, and stone. Brass dragons have fire breath, but prefer to use their sleep breath, as they don't like hurting anyone if they can help it.

Bronze Dragons: These dragons are very, very curious. They will shapeshift into more mundane animals in order to surreptitiously watch humans and other species go about their everyday business. Bronzes, like golds, have a very strong sense of justice and will go out of their way to fight evil and corruption wherever they find it. These dragons prefer to live along coastal areas or on islands. These dragons live in caves that are only accessible from under the water. The main cave, however, remains dry all the time. Bronzes have a series of eight horns around their head, three small ones along either cheek, two bigger ones on the top of the head, and a series of smaller horns running along the underside of the jaw. They have webbing between their forelimbs and feet, which aids in swimming. Bronzes eat mostly aquatic foods, and value shark meat above any other foodstuff. These dragons prefer treasures from the sea, such as pearls, coral, and amber. They will not fight unless they are left with no other choice. Instead, bronze dragons will find creative means to defeat an enemy without dealing fatal damage.

Copper Dragons: Coppers are the tricksters and pranksters of the dragonkin. They are also consummate riddlers and storytellers. Coppers prefer to live in mountainous areas. They live in narrow caves, the entrance to which is cleverly concealed. These dragons use magick to create wondrous, twisty mazes in their cavern homes. Copper dragons are powerful jumpers and climbers. They have blunt-muzzled faces with a pair of broad, flat horns on their heads and frills that flare out under their chins. Copper dragon wings are attached at the shoulders and run all the way down to right before the tip of the tail. This gives a flying copper the profile of a giant bat. Coppers will eat anything including metal ores, but their favorite foods are large poisonous creatures such as giant scorpions. In hoard building, coppers prefer treasures from the earth such as metals and precious jewels.

In addition to these basic dragon forms there are several more dragonkind in the world of *D&D.* The following is just a small sample.

Abyssal Drake: These creatures are the result of genetic experimentations gone horribly wrong. They are chimeric creatures combined of wyvern, demon, and red dragon. In appearance they favor the wyvern, having no fore-feet at all. They have serpentine necks, huge bat-like wings, and are scaled in black and dark red.

Dragonkin: These beings are humanoid distant cousins to the dragons. They are brutally strong and vicious. Dragonkin may be found in wild tribes or serving human masters. They stand 9 feet tall and have blunt-muzzled faces adorned with giant, frilled ears. Small horns hide in a mane of thick hair. Dragonkin have full-sized wings and a tail as well.

Dragonnel: These are dragon horses. They have ox-like bodies with dragon wings and a dragon tail. The head is a cross between an ox and a dragon with curling ram-like horns. Dragonell have hooved feet rather than clawed ones. They are hatched from eggs and are often trained as mounts for paladins and other special warriors.

Elemental Drakes: Most (but not all) drakes resemble wyverns. There are several different types of elemental drakes. **Fire Drakes** are wyvern-like, but are often mistaken for young red dragons. Fire drakes are the most evil of the drakes and enjoy being mistaken for their equally evil cousins. **Ice Drakes** are four-footed drakes with wings. They are scavengers that share territory with white dragons. These have ivory scales. **Air Drakes** look like the ice drakes, but with blue scales instead of ivory ones. They tend to be very cowardly and temperamental beings. **Earth Drakes** live up to the name drake indeed. These drakes have no wings at all, but have four sturdy feet with wicked claws. They are ponderous creatures, slow to anger but deadly if finally roused. They are rugged looking creatures with brownish scales. **Magma Drakes** look like wyverns in appearance. Their hide resembles cooling lava. They tend to live in volcanoes (obviously!) and particularly enjoy those with molten rock lakes or lava lakes. **Ooze Drakes** look like wyverns and are covered in viscous, caustic goo. They have slimy, gray-green scales and lamplight eyes. **Smoke Drakes** also resemble wyverns, but have decidedly bird-like snouts. They have smooth charcoal colored scales and glowing red eyes. **Water Drakes** have blue scales more fish-like than lizard-like in appearance. These drakes live on islands or along coastlines.

Faerie Dragons: These small dragons live in forests and tend to associate most often with fey creatures, such as pixies. They have platinum colored butterfly wings and a long prehensile tail that constantly twitches like a cat's tail. These dragon's colors resemble those of butterflies.

Fang Dragon: These draconic cousins have bony plate scales that have long spikes at the joints. The tail ends in double scythe blades. Fang dragons have stubby wings and do not fly well, but use the wings to get extra attacking thrust and momentum.

Landwyrms: The family of **landwyrms** are the ones that most resemble drakes. None of the landwyrms have wings. **Desert Landwyrms** are tawny in color and have webbing between the toes. Giant horns ring the head. They have long, serpentine bodies and are often mistaken for giant serpents until one is unlucky enough to get close and see its feet. These dragons are often called "tomb dragons" for their penchant for lairing in old tombs or ruins. **Forest Landwyrms** are noble protectors of the woods. They have mottled green-brown scales and a flattened frill around their necks that they may extend if they feel threatened so as to make themselves appear larger. **Hill Landwyrms** are russet red to light brown in color with huge tridactyl feet. These landwyrms are slow-witted bullies who enjoy picking on those weaker than themselves. **Jungle Landwyrms** are very saurian in appearance. They have emerald green scales with patches of red or yellow to help blend in with the lush jungle undergrowth. These landwyrms are pure evil; they know only hatred for all living things. **Mountain Landwyrms** are gigantic creatures that spend much of their time asleep or stationary. They resemble giant craggy rocks, and one might walk right past a sleeping one without ever realizing it. When one is awake however, the ground shakes with its passage. **Plains Landwyrms** are small but lethal scavengers. Like most scavengers they are cowards, but dangerous if cornered. They are tawny colored with stripes of yellow or tan to help them blend in on the plains. Halflings sometimes take the effort and time to train plains landwyrms as mounts. **Swamp Landwyrms** resemble Oriental dragons but do not share the temperament. They are vicious creatures that delight in tormenting other beings. Their green hide has frilled scales which are covered in a coating of slime and algae. Swamp landwyrms have webbed toes to help them swim through the muck of their homes. **Tundra Landwyrms** are a dirty ivory in color. They have giant, blunted claws to help them dig through frozen earth. Blunted spikes grace the chin, the nose, and the elbows/ankles. Giant rams horns adorn the head. These landwyrms spend a lot of time in a semi-hibernation burrowed under the frozen tundra.

Tiamat: The five-headed dragon god that rules the Plane of the Nine Hells. Each of her five heads is a different color, one for each of the Chaotic dragon species.

Bahamut: This platinum dragon is the King and Patron of all good dragons. He often chooses to take the form of a human and mingles with humanity.

Dragonlance

As with the original *D&D*, these dragons are broken up into chromatic dragons (which are usually evil dragons) and metallic dragons (which are usually good dragons). The chromatics were the first dragons created by the dragon god Paladine and the dwarf god Reorx. Unfortunately Takhisis stole them away and corrupted them. The metallic dragons were of the second batch of dragons created. These were supposed to serve as counters to the chromatics that Takhisis corrupted. These dragons live in the world of Krynn.

Black Dragons: These dragons are patently evil. They prefer swamps for homes and can breathe underwater. They are fiercely independent and were the most unreliable of dragons during the War of the Lance, frequently uncontrollable by their masters in the Dragon armies. Black dragons can see well in the dark. They will use darkness to blind and bind their foes.

Blue Dragons: Blues prefer deserts over any place else for homes. Blues are very social and cooperative. Of all the dragons, these are the ones most easily coaxed into working in a group. Working together, blues make very admirable opponents. Blues can use magick, but will likely turn to their electric breath weapon when fighting.

Green Dragons: These dragons are not so much fighters as diplomats and tricksters. They prefer using cunning rather than brute force when fighting. Greens are jealous treasure hoarders, and hoard away as much as they can find. These dragons can use magick or their deadly chlorine breath when fighting.

Red Dragons: These beasties live in the mountainous areas of Krynn and are even more the treasure hoarders than greens. Reds can use magick or utilize a fire breath attack. It is said that these great beasts can shapeshift into human form.

White Dragons: These dragons prefer the ice and tundra for their home. Smallest of all the chromatic dragons, they can be found near the Icewall Glacier. Whites can breathe out ice breath. Because whites live beneath the ice, they excel at breathing underwater.

Brass Dragons: Like their blue cousins, brass dragons prefer deserts and arid habitats for their homes. Brasses are of the opinion that "might makes right." However, they are not any more self-centered than any other dragon species. In a fight they will use a gas breath first, and turn to magick if that doesn't work.

Bronze Dragons: These dragons prefer to live near water, either fresh or saltwater. They utilize a lightning breath, much as the blues do. Bronzes dislike war and fighting and will avoid it at all costs. These dragons can use ESP to divine their enemies intentions, and thus evade them.

Copper Dragons: These are the smallest of the metallic dragons. Coppers prefer mountainous areas for their lairs. Of all the good dragons, these are the most self-centered of all. Coppers utilize a breath attack that slows opponents down. They will follow this with non-lethal spells. If all of that fails, they will turn a far more potent weapon upon their unlucky opponents—acid breath.

Gold Dragons: Like the coppers, the huge golds prefer mountainous areas for their homes. These dragons are the scholars and wizards of dragonkind. They are the ones most apt to keep huge libraries of books, much as their human counterparts do. Golds breathe fire just as the reds do, but they can also use a chlorine gas breath. Unlike most other dragon species, golds prefer to start with magick and use breath weapons only if their magick does not deter their opponent.

Silver Dragons: Silvers prefer the company of humans and demi-humans to that of other dragons. They will often live in or near human habitations. Silvers are gifted with the ability to shapeshift, which makes it very easy for them to blend in with these communities. Silvers utilize a paralysis breathe and ice breath to bring down opponents.

Sea Dragons: Sea dragons live beneath the waters of Krynn. They resemble nothing more than classical dragons crossed with giant frogs. Like frogs, they can breath

Sea Serpent Skeleton

both above the water and underwater. Sea dragons use a breath of superhot steam to dispatch those unlucky enough to get in their way.

Fire Dragons: These dragons are mockeries of real dragons. They are composed of red-hot lava. As such, it is not a very good idea to get too close to one. Fire dragons are evil creatures bent on destruction. Unlike other dragon species, fire dragons are weak magicians and rely more on brute force than magick.

Shadow Dragons: These dragons are not native to Krynn. Rather, they hail from the Plane of Shadows. These elusive dragons have translucent or opaque gray scales covering sleek, dark bodies. Shadow dragons excel at illusion spells and utilize a cone of shadow breath that drains victims of energy and strength. Shadow dragons are solitary creatures, preferring to keep to themselves.

Takhisis: This five-headed hydra dragon is the ruler of Hell. Takhisis is the equivalent to the *D&D* dragon-god Tiamat.

Paladine: The Dragonlance equivalent to Bahamut. This dragon is the Patron dragon god of all good dragons. He often chooses to wander the earth in the form of an absentminded old man named Fizban.

Forgotten Realms

Yet another subset of the world of *Dungeons and Dragons, Forgotten Realms* breaks dragons down in much the same way as its predecessors. Chromatic dragons lean towards the evil side and metallic ones to the good side of the spectrum. A bizarre group of people known as the *Cult of the Dragon* believe that dragons are destined to rule the world. At the top of this draconic power chain will be the undead dracolichs.

Red Dragons: Reds are the greediest of the *Forgotten Realms* dragons. They constantly seek to add to their great treasure hoards. These dragons are obsessed with wealth. Like Beowulf's fire drake, reds memorize their hoards down to the very last coin and gem. Red dragons utilize a fire-breath and can be very deadly foes. Unfortunately for them, these dragons are also very vain and conceited. Many a red has been brought down due to its ego.

Black Dragons: These dragons are among the most evil of dragon kind and the quickest to anger. Black dragons prefer dank and dark homes. Often they will choose to dwell in swamps or the depths of jungles, but sometimes they may be found deep underground. Black dragons are slightly less intelligent than their other kin, but that makes them no less deadly. They are worthy opponents for even the most seasoned adventurers. Black dragons utilize an acid breath that is extremely corrosive.

Blue Dragons: Blues are extremely territorial. They are so hostile to intruders in their territories that they will not rest until the intruder is no more than sun-bleached bones. Blue dragons prefer the hot, arid desert climates as their scales will blend easily with the never-ending blue of the sky. A blue dragon's scales, unlike other dragons, do not grow larger with the dragon. Rather, they stay the same size and grow harder and thicker. Blue dragons utilize a lightning breath attack.

White Dragons: These are the least intelligent of Faerun's draconic inhabitants. They are also the smallest. Though they may be small and slow-witted, the white dragons are among the most efficient hunters. White dragons give over to an instinctual rage when fighting, lending them great strength. These dragon prefer the coldest of climates: tundras, glaciers, and icepacks. The best places are those where the temperatures never rise above zero. These dragons will not eat anything that has not been frozen by its icy breath.

Green Dragons: Green dragons are all around bad-tempered, cruel, and rude. They hate all that is good and pure in the world, seeking to destroy it every chance they get. Greens will pick fights just because they are stronger than most other creatures. These dragons prefer to make their homes in forests. Like the blues, they are also very territorial beings. Green dragons fight using a toxic chlorine breath.

Yellow Dragons: These dragons are incredibly rare, preferring solitude to company. Yellows do not like to fight face to face. Instead, they lay cunning traps to capture their quarry. Yellow dragons live in deserts where the temperatures reach well above I00 degrees during the day.

Silver Dragons: These dragons are among the most kind and benevolent of Faerun's dragonkin. These dragons are the most likely to help humans in distress. Often, like their counterparts in *D&D* and *Dragonlance*, they will take the form of elderly men to travel among humans. A silver dragon may make its home in the high mountains, but more often than not they will live among humans in their assumed human forms.

Bronze Dragons: These dragons are fun-loving and easy going. A bronze's favorite past-time is changing into mundane forest creatures and following humans around to see if they do anything interesting. Bronzes are inquisitive and love contests, so long as they don't involve violence. These dragons prefer to make their home near bodies of water and are extremely good swimmers. Like blues, they also utilize a lightning breath attack. Bronzes, however, have a second card up their sleeve in the form of a foul breath attack that can drive opponents away without causing them harm.

Gold Dragons: Similar to the silvers, these dragons are among Faerun's kindest dragonkin. Like the bronzes, they can often be found traveling the world in the assumed form of an innocuous wild animal. They are very wise and judicious creatures. A gold hates nothing more in life than greed, injustice, and foul play. Gold dragons hate fighting, preferring to negotiate and talk things over whenever possible. If this is not possible, however, they are lethal fighters that utilize not only fire and toxic gas breath but magick as well.

Brine Dragons: These are truly the most bestial or feral of all the dragonkin. They have little intelligence and no family or social structure. They are fully aquatic animals, breaching the surface only to snag a bite to eat (such as unlucky sailors). These dragons are serpentine, with narrow heads and flippers in place of hands and feet. Brine dragons are very violent and unpredictable. Similar to turtles and other marine creatures, they leave their eggs to hatch on their own. The babies fend as best they can.

Dracolich: Only evil dragons can be turned into dracolichs. These dragons look much as they did in life, with the exception of glowing pinpoint lights in place of true eyes. The older a dracolich, the harder it is for it to maintain the preservation magick that holds the body together. They will take on a more skeletal appearance, as the magick is no longer able to hold scales and muscle to the bones. Dracolichs retain all of the abilities they had during life and gain the ability to paralyze a man with fear. Most dracolichs souls are held in phylacteries that are hidden. If such a phylactery is destroyed, the dragon will surely perish for good. Finding such a soul container is another matter altogether.

Rifts

In the realm of *Rifts*, dragons reach adulthood at roughly 600 years of age. They may live for several thousand years after reaching adulthood. Here, dragons are player characters as well as potential enemies. Even a weak dragon is more powerful than greater demons or supernatural beings, which is why so many primitive people worshipped them. The Rifts dragons get along well with humans for the most part. Many dragons have been among humans since they were hatchlings. Dragons, as with humans, run the gamut of alignments and ethics. All dragons, even the evil ones, prefer to be around humanoids, especially humans and elves. Dragons are fairly rare creatures. They are students of history, anthropology, literature, and sciences. They are adept in the use of technology and will use weapons, tools, optical enhancements, computers, and so on. Many of these dragons are also dedicated magick users and may even possess some poison skills as well.

A *Rifts* dragon tends to be greedy. They are known for hoarding artifacts, magick, and other valuables. They are also very strong physically and have an outstanding endurance. They may go without food or rest for great periods of time. Dragons can perform great feats of magick or keep up prolonged, intense activity for weeks at peak proficiency without food, rest, or even water. Eventually though, they will need to rest. At that point they may hibernate for weeks or even years.

Shapeshifting is a common natural ability and dragons enjoy disguising themselves. A favorite past-time is changing forms in the middle of a crowd and scaring people. *Rifts* dragons tend to be very loyal and true friends. They rarely betray or desert comrades. A dragon's wrath is a terrible thing, and oftentimes draconic justice is harsher than the crime would warrants.

Fire Dragons: These appear in many shades of red. They have massive wings and powerful limbs. Red dragons are most prolific in the use and study of magick. They can be found anywhere, but they prefer warmer climates over the colder ones.

Great Horned Dragons: These are the most feared and powerful of the Rifts dragons. They are master magick users. Standing 30 to 40 feet tall, with great, expansive wings, these dragons are impressive indeed. Great Horned Dragons vary in color from light green to golden orange.

Ice Dragons: These dragons are any shade of blue from light to dark and may sport white highlights. They can be found anywhere, but prefer the colder climates of glaciers and tundra.

Wind Serpent: These are long, serpentine, wingless dragons with copper, red/brown, or dark brown scales. They are greedy schemers and masters of subterfuge. Wind serpents are unrelenting in the pursuit of goals, and will do just about anything to achieve them.

Thunder Lizards: These are wingless gold/brown dragons. They are multi-dimensional travelers and avid magick learners/users. Thunder lizards are usually protectors of the downtrodden and the innocent. To see one of these rare, shy creatures is a sign of good luck.

Yu-Gi-Oh!

This popular card game (and anime series) sports a whole slew of dragons. The anime the game of *Duel Masters* is a card game, but with special technology developed by Kaiba Corporation, the monsters on the cards can come to life in a holographic form. The actual card game of *Yu-Gi-Oh!* is not yet able to harness such impressive technology, but is fun nevertheless. Listed here is just a small fraction of the ever growing number of dragon monsters in the game.

Baby Dragon: An orange-scaled baby classical dragon. Not very strong at first, but it has the potential to turn into a devastating monster.

Thousand Dragon: An ancient orange-scaled behemoth. This dragon is formed when a Baby Dragon and a Time Wizard are fused. The Thousand Dragon is a powerful monster.

Blue Eyes White Dragon: This extremely powerful silver-scaled dragon is the prime monster in Seto Kaiba's deck.

Blue Eyes Ultimate Dragon: Three Blue Eyes White Dragons can fuse into the supreme monster Blue Eyes Ultimate Dragon. This dragon has the same silver scales and brilliant sapphire eyes, but sports three heads instead of one! Both the Blue Eyes and the Blue Eyes Ultimate Dragons resemble bipedal classical dragons.

Red Eyes Black Dragon: Not quite as strong as the Blue Eyes White Dragon but every bit as impressive. The Red Eyes sports gleaming onyx scales and fiery red eyes. It is a bipedal classical dragon.

Red Eyes Metal Dragon: With the proper armor you can turn the Red Eyes into a dragon android!

Petite Dragon: A tiny winged serpent with little attack power.

Metal Dragon: This metallic dragon looks like the Chinese kiao. It sports a medium attack strength.

Winged Dragon, Guardian of the Fortress #1 and #2: These blue and red wyverns are of average strength. Each have blunted muzzles and stubby necks.

Blue Eyes Toon Dragon: This crazy little creature looks like a demented cartoon version of the Blue Eyes White Dragon. It has all the same features as its big brother, making it every bit as dangerous, no matter how cute it may look.

Spear Dragon: This wyvern has a long spear-like muzzle. It is so deadly that it can punch through defense monsters.

Luster Dragon 1 and 2: Made of emeralds and sapphires, these dragons are heavy hitters and good defenders. They are bipedal classical dragons with shimmering jewel-like scales.

Yamata Dragon: This dragon was patterned after the Yamata or Koshi dragon of Japanese legend. It has eight writhing heads and a fierce attitude.

Barrel Dragon: This draconic android sports a gun muzzle head and gun muzzle arms. Very powerful and dangerous, the Barrel Dragon has the added advantage of allowing a coin toss to decide if an opponent's monsters are destroyed before the battle phase.

Meteor Dragon: This tiny dragon looks like a walking meteor. Not very strong, but with the proper help it can become quite powerful.

Meteor Black Dragon: An upgraded and more powerful form of the Meteor Dragon. This dragon looks like it is made of cooling lava rock, giving it an interesting appearance.

Levia Dragon Daedalus: This sea serpent dragon can wipe a field of all monster cards save itself.

Chaos Emperor Dragon—Envoy of the End: Quite frankly, this is the most powerful dragon card in the game. It alone can completely wipe out a field, and both players hand cards while at the same time dealing massive damage to your opponent.

Pokemon

This popular Nintendo game has gone through many different incarnations, with each new expansion having more of the little "pocket monsters" added. Games in this series include *Pokemon Red/Blue, Pokemon Silver/Gold, Pokemon Yellow/Crystal, Pokemon FireRed/LeafGreen,* and *Pokemon Ruby/Sapphire/Emerald,* just to name a few. Many of the Pokemon are inspired by mythic creatures, and dragons are one of them. Dragon-type Pokemon are relatively rare, but Pokemon that resemble dragons are a bit more common.

Charmander/Charmeleon/Charizard: This trio of Pokemon are fire-breathing dragons. The final evolution, Charizard, resembles a classical dragon of Europe.

Onix/Steelix: While not dragon-type Pokemon, these creatures resemble great wurms of rock and steel.

Magikarp/Gyrados: This pair of Pokemon were inspired by the legends of the Dragon Gate in Asiatic myth. The first form, Magikarp, is a relatively week carp-like creature. However, if the Trainer sticks with it, this weak fish can evolve into the mighty Pokemon Gyrados. This giant sea serpent is scaled in sapphire and has catfish barbels on it's somewhat blunted snout.

Lapras: This water Pokemon is a sea turtle/dragon mix. Lapras look similar to the plesiosaur, with a spiky tortoise shell on its back.

Aerodactyl: This flying Pokemon is a wyvern. It has a dragonesque head, a pair of sturdy, bat-like wings, and two legs. Aerodactyl are incredibly rare.

Dratini/Dragonair/Dragonite: This trio of Pokemon start out as sleek sea serpents, but by the final phase they end up as peaceful, sleepy-looking classical dragons specializing in water-based attacks.

Lugia: This is a very rare flying Pokemon that resembles an overgrown wyvern. Lugia lives in the ocean and uses its great fan-like wings to propel it along underwater. Lugia can take to the skies as well, if it so chooses.

Torkoal: This fire Pokemon is a giant drake. It lacks wings, but has sharp claws on its feet and an excellent control of fire.

Vibrava/Flygon: This dragon-type Pokemon starts out life looking simiilar to an overgrown bug. But upon evolving, Vibrava turns into the faery dragon, Flygon.

Bagon/Shelgon/Salamance: This trio of Pokemon ends with a grand classical dragon. As with all other dragon-type Pokemon, these are very rare and hard to come by.

Rayquaza: This giant serpent dragon can fly without the aid of wings. He is very rare and very powerful. In appearance, Rayquaza has definite Meso-American traits.

Fire Emblem: Sacred Stones

Dragons in the Fire Emblem series usually make their appearance in the form of mounts for warriors called Wyvern Riders, and this game is no exception. Your basic Wyvern Rider has a mount that resembles the classical dragons. Wyvern Riders can be advanced to a Wyvern Knight or a Wyvern Lord with the proper training and tools. A Wyvern Knight actually does ride a wyvern mount. Wyvern Lords ride beefed up versions of the Wyvern Rider's mounts.

Creatures called Manaketes also exist in this version of *Fire Emblem*. Manaketes are dragonkin creatures. They look like humans except for having dragon wings. With a dragon stone the Manakete can turn into a full-fledged dragon.

Fire Emblem: Path of Radiance

The Wyvern Riders and Wyvern Lords make an appearance in the GameCube installment of the popular Fire Emblem series. These mounts are classical dragons that sport a spiky frill around their necks. Unlike the *Sacred Stones* Wyvern mounts, these are bipedal and have smaller hands and arms and more muscular legs. The only exception to this is King Ashnard's mount, Rajaion. This Wyvern looks more like the Wyvern Lord mounts of the *Sacred Stones* game.

Giant dragons also exist in the seclusion of the country of Goldoa. The Goldoan dragons live for centuries. One of two Goldoans will join your party later in the game—the White dragon Nasir or the Red dragon Ena. These dragons belong to a group of Were called Laguz. In addition to the Goldoan Dragons, there are the bird tribes of Kilvas, Serenes, and Phonecias, and the beast tribes of Gallia. All Laguz can take a human form, but there are traits that give them away. The Goldoans sport pointed ears, making them the most human looking of all. Beast Gallians sport cat tails and ears, and the bird tribes all sport wings in their human forms.

Final Fantasy

The ever -popular and long-running *Final Fantasy* (FF) series has long used dragons as both enemies and helpers. In most of the FF games, dragons of all forms are enemies. There are Oriental style dragons, classical drag-ons, wurms, and wyverns. Some of these include dragon zombies, grand dragons, red dragons, blue dragons, ruby dragons, azi dahakas, flame drakes, bolt drakes, ice drakes, claret dragons, greater drakes, vouivre, and chacs. In *Final Fantasy VII*, the pilot Cid can summon an oriental-style dragon as a special attack.

Ancient Drake

In addition, in most of the *FF* games dragons such as Tiamat, Bahamut, Neo Bahamut, Bahamut ZERO, and Leviathan can be summoned to aid in battle. Attacks with the word "dragon" in the name, such as Dragon Fang, Dragon Dive, Dragon Breath, Dragon Crest, and Six Dragons usually belong to older, wiser warriors, such as Cid Highwind of *Final Fantasy VII*, Freya of *Final Fantasy VIII*, and Sir Auron of *Finaly Fantasy X*.

Breath of Fire IV

The main character of all Breath of Fire games, Ryu, is a dragon or half-dragon child. In all of his incarnations, Ryu initially appears as a young boy or a teenager with distinctive blue hair. He rarely remembers his past or knows just what he is. As the story develops, he discovers his ability to change to full dragon or half-dragon forms, usually by traveling and speaking to different elemental dragons around the world. The best of the series, *Breath of Fire IV*, has a most unique story line. In this version, Ryu is one half of the Emperor Dragongod Fou-Lu. He was summoned into the world by incompetent magicians trying to raise the great Emperor Dragon. Ryu is Fou-Lu's nicer, softer side. Fou-Lu goes in search of his other half, and discovers that humans would love to kill him and use Ryu for the purpose of destruction. This angers the Emperor Dragongod so much that he vows to wipe out humanity after he has joined with his "other half." Ryu, however, finds much in humanity worth saving. It is up to the player which half will become the dominant one. Ryu spends much of the game traveling to speak to and learn from the Wind Dragon, Mud Dragon, Sand Dragon, Grass Dragon, Tree Dragon, Sea Dragon, and Rock Dragon. In his travels Ryu learns how to transform into various dragon forms, such as Aura Dragon, Kaiser Dragon, Wyvern, and Weyr. His dragon attributes are Flame-based. The player will switch between Ryu and Fou-Lu throughout the game. Fou-Lu has corresponding opposites in the Astral Dragon, Tyrant Dragon, Serpent Dragon, and Peist. His dragon attributes are Water-based. Once merged, Fou-Lu/Ryu becomes the Emperor Dragongod and can transform into the Yorea Dragon.

Lunar: Silver Star Story Complete and Lunar 2

Lunar: Silver Star Story revolves around dragons just as much as the aforementioned *Breath of Fire* series. The main character, Alex, seeks to follow in the footsteps of his hero Dyne and become a Dragonmaster. To do so he must seek out the Dragon Guardians and pass their tests. Each gives him gifts and helps him to grow spiritually. Alex must then help the dragons in defeating the Magic Emperor who seeks to overtake the world. The dragons of Lunar are ying-long, having fur and feathered wings. They may also take human form if they wish. Alex's longtime companion, Nall (who looks like a tiny flying cat), is actually a baby dragon—the dragon who will become the Quark's White Dragon replacement. This story is followed up by *Lunar II: Eternal Blue* in which another young man sets off to become a Dragonmaster. These events happen far in the future from the first story, but you still get to meet up with some old friends, such as Nall (now the White Dragon), all of the other dragon guardians, and the baby red dragon, Ruby, who has a penchant for breathing flames!

Spyro the Dragon Series

Spyro has spanned quite a few games on several different systems. The spunky purple classical dragon has collected gems and saved Dragon Realms on the PlayStation, PlayStation2, GameCube, Gameboy Advanced, and Nintendo DS. Spyro has sported both fire breath and ice breath. As with a great many dragons, Spyro is devoted to collecting all manner of gem-stones, hoarding them to gain access to different portals and realms.

Dragons in Film

Dragonheart

This 1996 movie starring Sean Connery ranks as one of the best dragon movies ever. In a rather unexpected move, the filmmakers decide to por-tray the European classical dragon, Draco, as a benevolent and good dragon—everything that a European dragon typically is not. Also atypical of European dragons, Draco sports a blunted muzzle, but otherwise fits the description traditional of classical dragons. While we do not get to see any other dragons, save the shadow of an old female, we are led to believe that Draco is an exception rather than a rule, and other dragons are evil.

Dragonheart: A New Beginning

This straight to video sequel to *Dragonheart* does not quite live up to its predecessor. However, it is not the worst movie out there. In the same atypical style of the first movie, it is the European dragon that is good and the Asiatic dragon that is evil. Drake, last of the European dragons left alive, must stop a human from using the preserved remnants of a dragon's heart to become a dragon himself.

Dungeons and Dragons: Wrath of the Dragongod

This *D&D* movie of 2005 did a much better job of keeping the dragons within the world of *D&D*. Of all the various dragon species, only two show up here. A white dragon, who is more than happy to show off his frost breath, and an ancient black dragon, the Dragongod of the title. For overall performance and script, this movie tops its predecessor in every way.

The Neverending Story

The Neverending Story is a 1984 movie featuring one of the most beloved dragons in film history. Falkor, the luck dragon, is based on the Asiatic fuku-ryu. Falkor flies without wings and sings with a bell-like voice. This great dragon has pearly white scales, a face that is a cross between cat and dog, and ruby red eyes. Always quick with a smile and words of good cheer, Falkor does great honor to the dragons he is based upon.

Mulan

Disney's hit film of 1998 features a small Chinese dragon by the name of Mushu (voiced by Eddie Murphy). Mushu is a tiny dragon in the kiohlung phase. Once a guardian to the Fa family, he was reduced to gong keeper after failing in his tasks. After accidentally destroying the guardian dragon statue, Mushu sets off to protect Mulan on her journey. This dragon is much smaller than his cousins, being only about the size of a house cat.

The Lord of the Rings

Based on The Lord of the Rings trilogy, this set of films by Peter Jackson feature some interesting dragons in the form of the Fell-Beast mounts of the Nazgul. They are giant wyvern-type creatures with a paralyzing gaze that can freeze men where they stand.

Reign of Fire

The dragons in Reign of Fire are wyverns. These beasts were sealed away long ago and have spent millenia slumbering beneath the earth's surface. Miners accidentally wake a pair of dragons who then breed. Soon enough, the monstrous beasts have taken over the planet and humanity has been thrown back into the Dark Ages. A group of people finally manage to figure out that there is only one male, part of the original pair. Taking him out will solve the dragon problem once and for all, but it isn't as easy as they'd like to think.

Dragonslayer

A 1981 movie that follows the standard medieval virgin sacrifice/heroic knight pattern. In this tale, the great dragon Vermithrax is terrorizing the countryside. At each equinox a virgin must be sacrificed to the dragon to stall its fury. Sacrifices are chosen by lottery, then staked out for the dragon's dinner. Villagers seek the aid of the sorcerer Ulrich. With the master sorcerer's seeming death, the task of dragon-slaying falls to his young apprentice Galen. For the time period this is not a half-bad dragon movie, though some might find it lacking in the special effects department.

The Cave

The creatures in this film of 2005, called demons in the beginning, actually look more like subterranean wyverns. They lack fore-feet, having only two hind-feet, and wing hands to walk quadrupedally. These underground creatures are the result of a parasite infecting a human host and mutating into a cave dwelling predator, thus ensuring the survival of both. They use sonar or echolocation to navigate and see, much as bats do. Their wings are fully functional, allowing them to glide across the vast underground caverns in the massive cave complex. They have blunt snouts and an interesting sonar apparatus on their heads, creating a type of crest. I will say that the movie is worth watching if you've not already seen it.

Spirited Away

This wonderful film of 2001, directed by the highly acclaimed Japanese director Hayao Miyazaki, features the dragon Haku/Kohaku. Haku has been tricked into serving Yubaba, running errands and helping to run the spirit bathhouse. Haku is a kiao-lung. He has no wings, but he can still fly. He has pearly white scales, eagle talons for feet, and a wolf-like head complete with horns and catfish barbels. Haku was once the spirit of the Kohaku River before humans drained it, filled it, and put apartments where the river once flowed. Due to human interference, Haku lost memory of who and what he was until Chihiro reminds him.

Harry Potter Series

This enchanting set of movies features a wide variety of dragons. It is in the first one, *Harry Potter and the Sorcerer's Stone,* that we are initially introduced to the dragons of Harry's world. This comes in the form of Norbert, a baby Norwegian Ridgeback hatched by the school's gamekeeper Hagrid. Norbert is a wyvern, brownish in color and with a distinctive ridge along the back. Next up is the basilisk from *Harry Potter and the Chamber of Secrets.* This dragon, unlike the most common descriptions of a basilisk, is a great and deadly wurm with a stony gaze. With the help of Fawkes the

Ancient Wyvern

phoenix Harry manages to defeat the evil creature. Lastly are the dragons of *Harry Potter and the Goblet of Fire.* In this movie you see tiny versions of a Swedish Shortsnout, a Welsh Green, and a Hungarian Horntail. The only dragon you get to see up close and personal is the Hungarian Horntail as Harry must face and defeat it. The Welsh Green and Swedish Shortsnout are classical dragons. We do not get to see a Chinese Fireball in the movie, though it is mentioned briefly. The Hungarian Horntail is reminiscent of Norbert, being a giant wyvern with a club knob at the end of its tail. Hungarian Horntails are known to sport bad tempers. The dragon animation here is wonderful. I only wish we got to see the other three dragons up close!

Fullmetal Alchemist

Dragons are prevalent in this series more as emblems than as actual beings. The Homunculi, those creations of human alchemy gone bad, all sport an Oroborus tattoo somewhere on their bodies. Sloth and Lust have them on their chests, and Gluttony has one on his tongue. Wrath sports one on the bottom of his left foot. Greed has his on the back of his hand, while Envy's is on the upper part of his left leg. Pride's is perhaps the most disturbing of all: it is on his right eye, which he normally wears a patch to cover. This tattoo is of a serpentine dragon having wings but no feet. Another type of dragon, the tatzelwurm, makes an appearance as the symbol for the State Military. This tatzelwurm rampant has a lion-head and a serpent body with a forked tail. The only living dragon to be found in this anime is in the form of Envy, one of the Homunculi. Envy is gifted with the ability to shapeshift, and at one point he turns into a massive emerald (representing green for envy) dragon patterned after the Asiatic kiao-lung dragons.

Saiyuki

Dragons have more of a role in the book which this series is based on than they do in this film. Nonetheless, they do show up. In the book *Journey to the West* the Tang Priest, Sanzang, has a dragon-turned-steed for a mount. In this modern adaptation the dragon mount shows up as well, in the form of a tiny white wyvern named Hakaryu. However, Hakaryu doesn't turn into a horse for Priest Sanzo; rather, he turns into a Jeep that the whole party can ride in!

Inuyasha

Dragons abound in this feudal fairy-tale anime. More often than not, Asiatic kiao-type dragons show up in the animae series as enemies. Inuyasha's half-brother, the wolf demon Sesshoumaru, also has a twin-headed dragon horse that serves to pull his aerial chariot.

Suggested for Further Viewing

- *Pete's Dragon*, 1977
- *Loch Ness*, 1996
- *Lair of the White Worm*, 1988
- *Flight of Dragons*, 1982
- *Dragonstorm*, 2004
- *Dragon Tales*, 1999
- *Pocket Dragon Adventures*, 1998
- *Dragonworld*, 1994
- *Godzilla*, 1998
- *Quest for Camelot*, 1998
- *Record of Lodoss War*, 1990
- *Dragonslayers*, 1981
- *Dragonhalf*, 1959
- *Sleeping Beauty*, 1959

* *Shrek*, 2001

* *Q-The Winged Serpent*, 1982

* *Dragon's World*, 2004

* *Dragonball Z*, 1989

* *Dungeons and Dragons*, 2000

* *Saiyuki*, 1978

Dragons in Literature

The Dragon Delasangre series by Alan Troop

The dragons of this wonderful series are shapeshifters that live among humans. There are four types, or castrylls: The Zal are the largest and are the fire-breathers; The Undrae are smaller than the Zal, but much smarter and they are skilled alchemists; The Pelk are the sea-dwelling dragons; and the Thyrll were the smallest of all and primarily live in tree-tops and hunt very small game. Today there are few of the People of the Blood, as they call themselves. Of the four groups, only the Undrae are still prevalent. Some Zal and Pelk still exist, but they are few and far between. The People of the Blood live for centuries. The Undrae, of which the Delasangres are a part, have green scales with pale, cream colored underbellies. They tend to walk bipedally and their dragon forms are usually twice the size of their human forms. Peter Delasangre, from whose point of view these stories are told, has a wingspan of 32 feet.

Dragon Quartet by Marjorie Kellogg

This series follows the four Draconic creators and maintainers of the planet and their Dragon Guides. First is Earth. Earth is a subterranean dragon who hates running water. He has a long serpentine body scaled in muted browns and greens. Two backswept ivory horns grace his head. In the beginning, Earth is much like a large puppy, but as time goes on he gains power and strength. Earth has the ability to heal with his tongue, to become invisible if still, and to teleport himself and those he knows to places that he or his Dragon Guide can picture. Earth's Dragon Guide is Erde Von Alte, a young noble lady of Germany. Water and her guide N'Doch show up next. Water is a sea dragon with a long, snake-like neck, four webbed feet, and a long, flat tail. She has a narrow head with seal-like ears and a small fin crest running down her neck. Water has silvery-blue fur that is as soft as velvet. From a distance it looks similar to fine fish scales. Water's gifts include the ability to shapeshift, to heal with her blood, and to "see" with sonar, as dolphins do. Where Earth communicates with images, Water communicates with music. N'Doch, Water's dragon guide, is a young African male of the year 2013. In a future even further distant than 2013, we meet the renegade dragon Fire and his guide Paia. Fire is a typical classical dragon with burnished coppery red scales. True to his name, one of his gifts is fire-breathing. Another of his gifts is the ability to take a human form, which, unlike his sister's, is insubstantial. He might look sleek and dapper, but he loses all of his ability to harm people. He can also time-travel. Fire is a manipulative dragon who has imprisoned the fourth elemental dragon, Air, and seeks to destroy Earth, Water, and their respective Dragon Guides. Fire's guide, Paia, serves as his High Priestess in a world where he is God and the End is coming. It's up to Earth, Water, Erde, and N'Doch to free their sister Air and stop their brother Fire before it's too late.

The War of the Lance Trilogy by Margaret Weis and Tracy Hickman

A number of specific dragons show up in this wonderful series by Weis and Hickman. Kisanth, a black dragon, has a sinuous, serpentine body, great leathery wings, and red eyes. Ivory horns grace her head. Kisanth travels to Ansalon for a time in the form of a beautiful human lady named Onyx.

During the War of the Lance, Queen Takhisis sends Kisanth to Xak Tsaroth to guard the Disks of Mishakal. Cyan Bloodbane is a great green dragon released from his prison at the end of the War of the Lance. He is promptly enslaved by the wizard Raistlin and used as a mount and servant for two years. Before being imprisoned, Cyan served Takhisis by responding to the Silvinesti dragon orb and corrupting the king's mind. Eventually the spell is broken and Cyan, driven off to Neraka, where he is later imprisoned by Takhisis. Matafleur is the ancient red dragon who guards the refugees at Pax Tharkas. She treats her charges more like children than prisoners. When the heroes arrive, Matafleur lets them go with little fuss, fearing harm will come to the refugees if she fights. Matafleur fights and defeats the red dragon Ember to prevent the younger red from killing the escaping refugees. Silvara is a gentle silver dragon. A friend of elves and a great healer, it is she that leads the Heroes to find the dragonlances and gives them the knowledge to make more. There are a great many more dragons in the *War of the Lance* series and a great many more books in the whole *Dragonlance* series, each with fascinating dragons and other mythical, magickal creatures to meet. If you love dragons and love reading, travel the world of Krynn. No doubt you will find many new friends!

The Hobbit by J.R.R. Tolkien

Smaug is probably one of the best known of the modern dragons. He is a reddish-gold dragon with an evil temper. Smaug lays waste to the town of Dale and captures the Lonely Mountain with all of its treasures. Like so many dragons world-wide, Smaug keeps adding to his already huge hoard. Despite this he keeps and knows every single coin and gem. Smaug has lain upon his treasure hoard for so long that his belly is covered with scales that shine like gems. However, when the hobbit Bilbo Baggins confronts the great dragon, he discovers a small spot free of gems; the dragon's weak spot. This weakness eventually leads to his downfall when an archer strikes and kills him.

Dragon's Winter/Dragon's Treasure by Elizabeth Lynn

Dragons, in Lynn's wonderful world, are all changlings. They have a human form and a dragon form. Changlings are born of at least one human parent, but in the case of dragon changlings, a human mother will often perish in the birthing of the child. A baby dragon changling will have tiny claws in place of fingernails, which slough off shortly after birth. All changlings grow fast, far surpassing their human age-mates in size and intelligence. Karadur Atani, the Golden Dragon, is a wyvern in appearance. He has shimmering golden scales and eyes like molten fire. Dragons are among the most unstable of the changling races. They can anger without a moment's notice, and do considerable damage during their fits of rage. It is in such a rage that Karadur Atani's father, Kojiro the Black Dragon, destroys the city of Mako. Years later, a similar fit of rage causes Karadur to destroy the Lord of Silvano's home. Thankfully, this dragon keeps enough control of himself to not destroy the whole town.

The Icewind Dale Trilogy by R.A. Salvatore

Similar to the novels of the popular Forgotten Realms subset of *D&D*, this series has plenty of dragons. While Salvatore is better known for his creation of the dark elf ranger Drizzt Do'Urden, his dragons are no less fascinating and memorable. In the Icewind Dale trilogy we are introduced to the white dragon Icingdeath. Drizzt fights this fearsome dragon with his friend Wulfgar. The barbarian finally dispatches the great dragon by causing a huge icicle to fall from the ceiling and impale the dragon. Later, during the group's efforts to regain the lost dwarven stronghold of Mithril Hall, we meet the shadow dragon Shimmergloom. This great wyrm is finally slain by Bruenor Battlehammer, the rightful dwarven heir to Mithril Hall.

The Dark Elf Trilogy by R.A. Salvatore

Perhaps the funniest encounter that the dark elf Drizzt has with a dragon occurs in this series. While traveling with a group of humans, he passes through the lair of Hephaestus, a venerable red dragon living in a cave west of the town of Miribar. Drizzt approaches Hephaestus claiming to be the black dragon Mergandevinasander. This black dragon is known for having purple eyes, which happens to be one of Drizzt's unique features as well. Playing on the red's vanity, Drizzt tricks him into breathing fire for an extended period of time, giving the humans enough time to cross the dragon's lair unseen.

Cleric Quintet by R.A. Salvatore

In this series, Salvatore leaves the adventures of the dark elf ranger, Drizzt Do'Urden. Instead he takes us on a journey with Cadderly Bonaduce. During this priest's journeys, he tricks the red dragon Feyrentennimar into serving as a mount in an effort to get out of the Snowflake Mountains quickly.

Dragon Knight Series by Gordon R. Dickson

This series is highly readable and enjoyable. Sir James Eckert, once Jim Eckert, college professor, is thrown back in time due to a science experiment gone wrong. Initially his soul ends up in the body of the dragon Gorbash. Later, when Jim is finally human again, he learns to turn into a dragon himself. Jim is an apprentice magician of the Baron of Malencontri. He is also known as the Dragon Knight, due to his ability to shift shape. The dragons of this world are classical dragons in appearance, though wyverns, wurms, and sea serpents do make appearances throughout the series. Dragons, and their stunted cousins the mere-dragons, stand bipedally when on the ground. They are lazy, placid creatures, but fearsome when angered. These dragons can't swim, for they are heavier than water. They sink faster than a stone! As with so many other dragons, these create hoards and guard them jealously. In Dickson's medieval world, dragons call humans "georges."

The Dragonriders of Pern Series by Anne McCafferey

The dragons of Pern are genetically engineered creatures specifically designed to fight the scourge of Thread. They are created from the native fire-lizards. Both species resemble classical dragons. Pernese dragons have multifaceted eyes that change colors depending on their moods. They can breathe fire by ingesting firestone, and they can communicate with each other and with their bonded human telepathically. Dragons are bonded to a human, their Dragonrider, from the moment they are hatched. These dragons come in several different colors. Golds are always female and tend to be the rarest of all. Next are bronzes who are always male. Next to the golds, they are the largest of the dragonkin. Bronzes usually (but not always) father the gold's clutches. Next in size are the male browns, followed by the blues. Last, but not least are the greens, the smallest of Pern's dragons.

Faniuhl by Daniel Hood

Faniuhl, the star of the *Faniuhl* series is a tiny classical dragon about the size of the house cat. The dragon is a wizard's familiar, and as such is tied to the wizard by taking a pierce of his or her soul. Faniuhl can let the wizard see through his own eyes, making him a good scout. He also enhances magickal workings and can perform small magicks himself. Faniuhl is a telepathic beast, talking to its master mind to mind. Faniuhl is familiar to Liam quite by accident. When his previous wizard master was brutally murdered, the tiny dragon latched on to the next person to come along in order to survive.

Mistress of Dragons by Margaret Weis

Dragons in this world resemble the classical dragons of Europe. They come in all kinds of colors. Draconas, a draconic walker, or dragon in human form, is actually a beautiful red-scaled dragon. Dragons of the Dragonvarld are forbidden to interfere with the lives and affairs of humans. Yet a rogue dragon has isolated herself in a human kingdom, where she trains females to fight using dragonmagick. She ships young boys out to be food for her partner or to be trained in dragon magick.

The Loch by Steve Alten

Alten's main focus is the Loch Ness monster, that most famous of water dragons. This book takes a scientific look at Nessie, putting forth the theory that she/it is not a remnant dinosaur, but a precursor species to a more modern sea dragon, the Anguilla eel. A highly enjoyable read, full of just as much magick as science.

Suggested for Further Reading

- *Elvenbane* by Mercedes Lackey and Andre Norton, Tor Books, 1993
- *Dragon Jouster's Trilogy* by Mercedes Lackey, Daw Books, 2006
- *The Last Dragonlord* by Joanne Bertin, Tor Books, 1999
- *Dragon and Phoenix* by Joanne Bertin, Tor Books, 2000
- *The Pit Dragon Trilogy* by Jane Yolen, Magic Carpet Books, 2005
- *The Deathgate Cycle* by Margaret Weis, Bantam Del Pub Group, 1990
- *Dragon World* by Bryon Priess, I Books, 2002
- *Eragon/Eldest* by Christopher Paolini, Knopf Books, 2004
- *Eddie's Blue Winged Dragon* by C. S. Adler, Backinprint.com, 2004
- *Voyage of the Dawn Treader* by C. S. Lewis, HarperTrophy, 1994
- *His Majesty's Dragon* by Naomi Novik, Del Ray, 2006

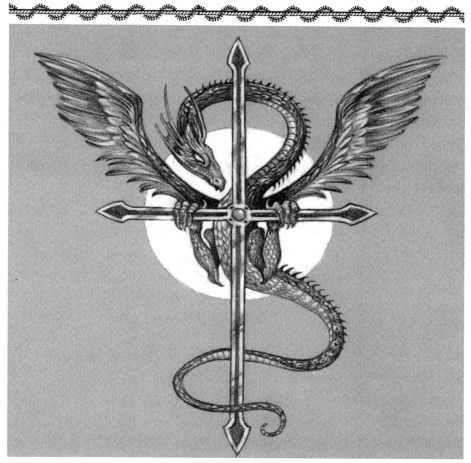

Original Dragonlore

Dragon Jewels Part One: Into the Dragonlands

By Wolfsong

The Dragon Priests

A breeze blew through the trees, ruffling the young Dunne'kaa's hair. She was a petite female, with jet black hair and a single emerald eye. Where the other eye should have been the lids were sealed shut. A thin scar ran from her forehead down to her cheek, the price she had paid to be

Grael's Priest. She was dressed in the traditional raiment of a Dragon Priest, golden robes with a snarling dragon climbing up the back. Her purple trimmed Sumatra stole rested on her shoulders, fluttering in the breeze, and the amethyst dragon jewel glittered where it peeked through her hair. The Dragon Priest lifted her head, enjoying the feel of the wind on her face and turned to her companion.

"Dart'aan. We should start looking for a place to camp tonight. There's rain in this wind. A storm's coming."

"Eh?" The other Dunne'kaa, a tall male with dark brown eyes and sandy brown hair, turned to look at her, his contemplative mood broken. He wore light brown robes, the collar trimmed in silver marking him as part of Bahamut's sect. He was a monk of the Dragon Temple, traveling with her to Bear Clan territory. Many of the Dragon Priests and the Temple monks had been summoned to this furthermost territory of Dunn'Mar to deal with human invaders, Dart'aan and D'Challya among them. Dart'aan tilted his head, testing the wind for himself. "Aye, Mistress. That we should." He fell silent, returning to his quiet thinking.

D'Challya shook her head, wondering what her companion was thinking about. Probably the same thing she had been dwelling on. Human invaders in the Dragon Lands. Human invaders who could kill the Dragon Priests, those few blessed by the Dragon Patrons themselves. At any given time there were only 11 Dragon Priests. One for Grael, Ayahz, and Bahamut and two each for Gaia, Rai, Freyeth, and Tiamat. The Patrons themselves chose the replacements when a Priest passed on. That was how she had been elevated, not six months prior, when M'Karr had fallen fighting the forerunners of the invaders. And only last week another had been killed— the Earth Priest San'zo. All of the Priests could feel the loss through their connections to the Patrons. She had met the Earth Priest once, shortly after she had been raised. He had been a quiet, gentle-natured fellow, as unassuming and shy as the Patron he served. While Grael had wasted no time in replacing the fallen M'Karr, no new Earth Priest had been raised. D'Challya wondered what Gaia was waiting for. And for that matter, how could the humans possibly kill two of the Dragon Priests? Each priest had a lesser dragon spirit helper, tied to them through the Sumatra stoles they wore. And they could wield powerful dragon magic through the stones in their foreheads, the dragon jewels. Not to mention that all Priests (and monks) were excellent fighters, trained in hand-to-hand combat and a wide assortment of weaponry. So what could possibly take out not one, but two Priests?

Lost in their own thoughts the pair continued to follow the track of the river until they came across a small clearing nestled against the bank. Here they decided to stop for the night and D'Challya shielded their campsite with magic to keep the rain out.

After dinner they sat around the fire, listening to the rain patter on the shield and the rumble of thunder in the distance, talking of tomorrow.

"We should reach the outskirts of Bear Clan territory tomorrow midday. Bahamut willing, we will make contact with another of the Priests. Or with some more Temple monks. Although, I'd like to meet some of these humans. I'm itching for a good fight."

"Tch. Who's the child of the Wardragon here? Though I agree. I'd like a little revenge myself. And Azhi hungers for blood." D'Challya smiled, thinking of the dragon spirit that had chosen to be hers: Azhi Dahaki, the demon dragon, and one of the strongest black dragon spirits. When a new Priest is chosen, they begin making their own Sumatra stoles, embroidered with a spirit binding spell. A dragon spirit chooses their own master and influences the making of the Sumatra, each spell specific to one particular dragon spirit. And Azhi had chosen her. The demon dragon who had called no one master for nearly 2,000 years. As she thought of him, D'Challya felt the demon dragon's mind slip through hers. A brief touch as he tested how she was feeling. The blood hunger grew stronger, then faded.

"We should sleep now Mistress. We have a long day ahead of us. Can't let everyone else have all the fun now can we?" Dart'aan's voice broke through her thoughts and she grinned at him.

"No. No, we certainly can't. Goodnight Dart." She settled back, covering herself with her cloak, but it was a long time before she was able to drift off to sleep.

The next day dawned bright and cold. Both monk and Priest rose with the sun. They ate a quick breakfast, packed up, and broke camp. Several hours passed in easy, uninterrupted travel. *I smell blood Mistress, fresh blood. Dunne'kaa blood. And humans too.* Azhi's voice sounded in her head just as Dart'aan stopped walking, motioning for her to stop as well. She sniffed, checking the winds with Dart'aan. What she smelled confirmed what the demon dragon had told her. Dunne'kaa blood. And the stench of humans. She snarled low in her throat, baring wicked fangs.

"Looks like we'll get our fight today after all Mistress."

"Aye, Dart. That we will. That we will." The pair melted into the forest, creeping towards the smell of humans until they came to a large clearing. D'Challya cloaked the two of them in dragon magic to shield them from view, then added a shield to prevent damage.

Humans filled the clearing, tents and people everywhere. D'Challya snarled to herself, her innate bloodlust filling her. Filthy humans. How dare they come here and destroy her lands, her people. The pair edged closer, making their way around the camp. Dart'aan inhaled suddenly and growled deep in his throat, pointing to the far side of the clearing. She followed his finger, her eye coming to rest on a small, gold bundle that a group of humans surrounded, taking turns kicking it. One reached down and pulled the limp bundle halfway off the ground. He shook it, and seemed to be talking to it. She made out gold robes with a darker gold dragon winding up the back. The clothes of a Dragon Priest. The human let the bundle fall back down, giving her a better look. He had a mane of blond hair and his eyes were closed. Earth Priest, San'zo! But how? Blood roared in her head and faintly she heard Azhi's voice...*I hunger Mistress. Free me. Let us dance with Carron and have our revenge.*

D'Challya burst forward from cover, dissolving the invisibility shields and calling Azhi to her. The wind howled around her as the demon dragon heeded her summons. Her wild charge into the camp had scattered the humans, but now they closed around her. Nearby she could hear Dart'aan, twin swords cutting a swathe through his opponents. She grinned, a mad glint in her eye. The demon dragon's great obsidian body shimmered darkly in the sunlight, his red eyes glittering with ruby malice. A pair of rams horns curled back over horse-like ears. A black mane ran down the demon dragon's back and fur tufted his ankles and elbows as well. Foot-long spikes adorned his lashing tail. Azhi roared and plowed through the crowd, snapping up humans and crushing them in powerful jaws. D'Challya turned to those still facing her, maybe thinking the diminutive Dragon Priest easy prey since she held no weapons and her dragon had run off. She snorted. They had no idea that of the two Dunne'kaa she was the more dangerous, not Dart'aan. Only the finest and most vicious fighters belonged to Grael's sect. And only the best of those was Grael's Priest. One of the humans lunged at her, swinging wildly with his sword. With a movement swifter than the clumsy human's she ducked the blow, at the same time drawing out her kappen. In the right hands the bladed fans were very dangerous weapons, but they required close combat. She continued forward, bringing herself closer to her opponent. She snapped one of the fans open and sliced upward, slitting his throat, then danced back out of the way of the falling body. D'Challya smiled grimly as blood spattered against her shields and she gave full rein to the bloodlust, entering what a human might call a berserker's fury. But unlike human berserkers she never lost complete control of who she was and what she was doing.

The Shadow Priest danced among the humans, leaving a trail of bodies to mark her passage. Dart'aan caught glimpses of D'Challya while he was fighting. He shivered, almost feeling sorry for the humans who had to face her. Within minutes, monk, dragon, and Priest had decimated the entire human camp. Dart'aan turned to his companion, watching as the blood fury diminished.

"Vengance is good, Mistress. But I am troubled. These humans were no match for us, so how could they have captured San'zo and incapacitated him? Even the most passive of Priests can be a force to be reckoned with if angered." Dart'aan's voice was full of the contempt he felt for the humans.

'I know, I know. Let us go see to San'zo and he can tell us himself."

D'Challya flicked blood off the kappen, snapped them shut, and made her way across the camp to where the Priest lay in a heap, monk and dragon following behind. She frowned as she looked down on the Priest, cold fury settling itself around her like a blanket. San'zo had been severely beaten. Blood covered his tattered robes, his face was bruised and swollen, and a strange collar was fitted about his neck. Made of a metal she had never seen before, it didn't appear to have any seams to show where it could be removed. She knelt down and gently pushed the Earth Priest over onto his back. At her touch he shivered violently and curled back up on his side without opening his eyes. By Grael's teeth, what had happened to him?

"San'zo? San'zo, we're here to help you. We're not going to hurt you. My name is D'Challya. I'm Grael's Priest. We've met before, though you might not remember me." *Mistress? I cannot feel the Earth Priest, nor can I feel his draconic guardian. I do not understand. I see him here, but everything else tells me he should be dead.* Azhi's voice rumbled through her head, his words adding to her own confusion. She had felt the loss of the Priest, yet here he was alive, if not quite well. He was shaking and it took her a moment to realize that he was sobbing silently. In an uncharacteristic gesture she pulled the Priest up into her lap and he buried his head against her, fingers knotting her robes. He was sobbing openly now. She rocked him gently, making shushing noises, as if to calm a fretful child. Dart'aan came and knelt beside her, a quizzical look on his face and she gave a small shake of her head.

Dart'aan was amazed. D'Challya, like himself, normally shunned any kind of prolonged contact with another person. He couldn't recall her ever offering comfort to another either, though both had seen worse than this. As he watched her, Dart'aan noticed that the perpetual harshness had left her face. As she was now, the Shadow Priest looked like nothing less than a mother comforting a child. It was very odd, very disconcerting. Dart'aan started to say something, but was cut off by the Earth Priest's soft voice.

"Gone...all gone....can't feel her anymore. The collar...cuts me off from her." San'zo's voice was muffled by D'Challya's robes, but the anguish in his voice was clear enough. He had quieted down somewhat, but still had a death grip on her robes, fingers wound so tight that she was surprised his

claws hadn't torn the fabric. She frowned. The only "her" that he would be cut off from was Gaia, his Patron dragon. And his dragon guardian. The collar cut him off? How was that possible? She used her free hand to brush his hair away from the back of the collar, then placed her hand against it. Pain seared through her, then...nothing. A complete emptiness and an almost unbearable loneliness. She heard Azhi roar in frustration and confusion. D'Challya jerked her hand away from the collar and tried to catch her breath. What magic was this? What kind of metal could possible disrupt the connection between Priest and Patron/guardian so completely? *DON'T DO THAT AGAIN!* Azhi's roar filled her head, bringing her back to her senses. "Okay, okay. I don't plan on it Azhi. Don't shout." *Hmph. See that you don't. You had me scared. I couldn't feel you. Our connection flickered and vanished.*

Poor guy. He's felt that loss for nigh on a week now. As has his guardian.

Rise of a Priest

D'Challya stayed with the Earth Priest while Dart'aan searched the camp. Soon enough he found San'zo's belongings, his pack with spare clothing, and his staff. When he returned to the Priest's side he found San'zo asleep and D'Challya with a worried look on her face.

"Dart, we need to get him cleaned up and taken care of. But not here. We should return to the river and set camp. San'zo isn't in any condition to be doing much traveling right now. And maybe we can find a way to free him."

"Aye, Mistress." Dart'aan lay the pack and staff on the ground, then stooped to pick the Earth Priest up. He was startled at how light San'zo was. He frowned and looked at D'Challya, who met his worried gaze with one of her own. The Shadow Priest collected San'zo's belongings and the pair of them made their way back to the river, finding a suitable area for a campsite.

Evening found San'zo awake, if somewhat listless. They had gotten him cleaned up and looking much better than he had been before. Feeling better was another story altogether. San'zo felt like he no longer qualified as a Dragon Priest anymore. His depression was almost tangible. He kept his gaze to the ground, refusing to meet either the monk or Priest's eyes. He talked very little and only if spoken to. D'Challya had, however, managed to get out of him how he had been captured. He had been shot with an arrow of the same material as the collar, which had disrupted his magic. After that the humans' sheer numbers had pulled him down and he had been collared.

D'Challya was worried about San'zo. The Earth Priest had eaten very little for dinner, and it was doubtful he'd had decent food during his captivity. He no longer had the will to live. He had given up and she was afraid of what he might do to himself. She couldn't imagine having to live without her magic, without Grael, without Azhi. Though both she and Dart'aan had tried, they had been unable to get the collar off.

San'zo had disappeared into the woods shortly after dinner and Dart'aan had silently followed after him. Time passed and just when she thought she was going to have to go after them, Dart'aan returned. He nodded to her.

"He's fine. He should be back in a bit. He went down to the river and sat on the bank. I don't know what he was contemplating, but he's coming back now." D'Challya sighed, partially in relief and partially in frustration. She hoped they found a way to remove the collar soon, to give the Earth Priest back all that he'd lost.

San'zo made his way slowly back to the camp, lethargy and despair dragging his every step. He'd gone to the river, hoping to find the courage to do what he knew he should do, but he hadn't found it. He didn't want to live any more, not like this. But he didn't have the guts to end it. He knew the Shadow Priest and the monk didn't need to be burdened with him. He'd only be a hindrance to them. He sighed. Maybe tomorrow.

San'zo entered the camp and made his way slowly over to D'Challya. He didn't know why but he felt safest near the Shadow Priest and a little less depressed. He knew she probably despised him being close to her. All of Grael's children were like that, hating to have others close to them. But the Earth Priest sincerely hoped that she wouldn't drive him away. He needed what little comfort he could find at the moment. He dropped to his knees in front of her, folding his hands in his lap.

"Please Mistress, may I stay near you tonight? I...I feel safe with you, something I haven't felt for quite some time." His gaze flicked up and found her staring intently at him. Just when he thought she would refuse, she nodded. "You may."

She gestured to where she sat by her bedding, inviting him to curl up next to her. He gave her a grateful look and settled down. When they were both comfortable D'Challya threw her cloak over the pair of them and tried to get some sleep. She hadn't had the heart to refuse the Earth Priest's request, but his closeness did make her uncomfortable, though she would never let him know that. If being near her could give him any measure of comfort then she wouldn't turn him away.

Dart'aan smiled to himself as he watched the two Priests. He hadn't seen D'Challya act so...caring before. He strongly suspected that the Shadow Priest felt *something* for San'zo, though what exactly he wasn't sure. It was very rare for one of Grael's children to love another. Even rarer was the Graelen who took a mate. D'Challya, herself, probably wasn't aware of her feelings and would have vehemenetly denied it if made aware. Dart'aan decided not to say anything and see what happened. He did wonder what it was about the Gaian that had sparked her unconscious interest, and so quickly at that. Something to ponder at a later time. Chuckling quietly to himself, the monk curled up in his own blankets and soon fell asleep.

The next morning Dart'aan and D'Challya were discussing what they should do to help the Earth Priest, when Azhi's agitated voice interrupted them.

MISTRESS! GO TO THE RIVER. QUICKLY! D'Challya jerked her head up. The river? San'zo had gone to the river earlier, as he had the night before. And as before Dart'aan had followed him and left him sitting by the bank, lost in thought. What could possibly have happened to him? D'Challya had a sinking feeling she knew the truth of the matter and sorely wished she'd had Dart'aan stay with him. She jumped up and took off running, a confused Dart'aan following behind her. She ran, letting Azhi guide her. They reached the river and found nothing. *Here, here. In the water. Go in the water.* Azhi's voice was insistent so she quickly unbelted the robe and pulled it off, leaving her in the lightweight supter pants and shirt that the monks wore under their robes. She dropped the robe and her Sumatra stole on the bank and dove into the frigid river. It was a good thing she preferred the cold or the water might have made her pass out from shock. She swam in the murky water, unable to see, trusting in the demon dragon's directions. Her hands touched something soft, her fears confirmed. She grabbed a handful of cloth and started back to the surface, pulling her heavy load along.

Reaching the riverbank she pulled San'zo out of the water. Dart'aan reached over to help and together they pulled the Earth Priest's limp body up onto the bank. She turned him over and saw what had made him so heavy. He had weighted the voluminous pockets of the robe down with river rocks, making sure he would sink to the bottom. The Earth Priest was freezing cold and already turning blue. He wasn't breathing and he had but a faint heartbeat. She tilted his head back and blew into his mouth, filling his lungs with air. Once, twice, and then he coughed, struggling to breath on his own. D'Challya pulled the Earth Priest over on his side while he coughed up all the water he'd swallowed. Then she used her dragon magic to dry the two of them off, leeching the water out of their clothing. He lay for a minute on his side, breathing heavily.

"Why? Why did you save me? Why didn't you just let me die?" His voice was so soft she almost didn't hear him.

"What kind of a question is that Earth Priest?" She said with a faint shake of her head.

"Let me go. A replacement has more than likely already been found. I'm a Dragon Priest no longer. I don't want to live like this for the rest of my life, knowing what I had and what I've lost. You felt it, for a moment. Could you stand to feel like that for the rest of your life?"

She paused, frowning. No, she wouldn't want to feel like that for the rest of her life. Suicide would probably be her choice, too. She sighed.

"Fine, give us a week to see if we can free you from the collar. If not, then I will...assist...you in your death. The poison that tips my crossbow bolts will put you in a sleep you won't wake up from."

"Three days. No more. You won't be able to get the collar off anyway." A heaviness filled her chest. She didn't want him dead, and certainly didn't want to assist in that death. D'Challya shook her head. Since when had she grown so soft-hearted. San'zo was right, a replacement hadn't been found yet, but if he died in truth then a new Earth Priest would be raised. The only reason he hadn't already been replaced was because he *was* still alive. Why should she care if he lived or died? She never would have before; why should she now? Why was she losing her sensibilities when it came to dealing with San'zo? No, why should she care indeed? "Trust no one, care for no one"—that was a mantra she'd long lived by. She snarled softly.

"Very well, three days. No more." Her tone was gruff and San'zo flinched at her harshness.

"Thank you, Mistress." She snorted as she gathered up her stuff. D'Challya stalked back up the path, leaving an uncertain Dart'aan to gather up the fallen Priest and bring him back to the camp.

Later, Dart'aan found D'Challya further past the camp, practicing with her kappen. He had left the Earth Priest in the camp, telling him that maybe, just maybe, San'zo had come to mean more to D'Challya than just being another Dragon Priest. Though for the life of him, he didn't know how. He grinned, thinking of the shocked look on the other's face as he left.

Dart'aan could tell by her movements that D'Challya was very agitated, though she would never admit it. He smiled, chuckling to himself. Someone, for whatever reason, had finally cracked the shell around the Shadow Priest's heart and she didn't know how to deal with it. Now she struggled to rebuild that shell, not knowing how to fix it and probably not

knowing why it was broken in the first place. That could be a good thing though. Maybe caring for San'zo would soften some of her harshness and temper her sometimes overly-pessimistic nature. Maybe this was all part of one of Grael's divine plans, to test and strengthen her Priest. Maybe. And maybe mokras would fly.

"Mara sou, Mistress." D'Challya spun around, bringing the opened kappen into a guard position. She glared at him across the clearing.

"What do you want Dart'aan? Go away and leave me be."

"No, Mistress. I don't think that's so wise." Dart'aan had stopped on the edge of the clearing, not daring to go any closer to the volitale Shadow Priest. He doubted he could beat her with weapons, good as he was, and if she grew too angry with him there was no way he could fight dragon magic. Or Azhi for that matter. And the demon dragon would have little compunction at following her orders. Oh, the spirit dragon would never kill him, a Dunne'kaa monk, but he would certainly administer discipline if the Priest ordered it.

"You care for him don't you? The Earth Priest, that is."

"Don't be ridiculous, monk. I couldn't care less. Now go away," she snarled at him. Hmm, not good. She'd stopped using his name. Being called monk by one of the Priests was never good, and that doubly applied to D'Challya. It meant they were very, very angry. Maybe this hadn't been such a good idea after all. But he was here now, and it wasn't in him to turn and run. No matter that it may have been the wiser course of action.

"Ne, Mistress. The D'Challya who couldn't care less would have killed him there on the riverbank and not thought anything about it. Face it Mistress. You care for him and don't want to assist in his death."

"You...know...nothing...monk. And you forget your place," she stalked across the clearing towards him, fury growing with her every step. Dart'aan held his ground, not backing away from the furious Priest.

"I do know some things Mistress. And I have not forgotten my place. That place is by your side, helping you. And I'd say you need help now, to see your true feelings. Is it really so unbelievable that you can't even admit that you might actually care for him?" He cringed inside. Was he mad? He didn't think he had a death wish, but he must to continue this confrontation.

"Trust no one monk. Care for no one. That's the safest bet you will ever make. Besides, even if I did care, which I don't, does it really matter? The Earth Priest wants to die. That kind of makes it a moot point now doesn't it?" She stopped in front of him, a defiant look in her eye.

"You trust me, don't you?" He favored D'Challya with a wounded look, spreading his hands wide and she faltered, losing some of her anger. "I think, Mistress, that he would be very surprised to learn that you care about him, and knowing would change how he feels about dying. Wouldn't you agree? "

"Trust you? No, I don't trust you, you manipulative bastard." A slight grin belied her harsh words and her anger slowly drained away. "Fine, fine. I give up. No, I don't want to see him dead, nor do I really want to help that death along." She paused for a moment, considering Dart'aan's words. "Yes, I think maybe I do care about him." Uncertainty flooded her face and he could see that she was still trying to talk herself out of this seeming weakness.

"Then you should tell him how you feel, Mistress. Caring for someone makes you no less of a Grael's Priest. It is my considered opinion that what you both need is something to care about, or someone to care for. San'zo especially. He needs another reason to keep living, so why not you? Go back and talk to him. I'll just...uhh...practice here for awhile."

"Your 'considered' opinion, huh? Very well," she sighed. She started to walk off, robes swirling around her, then stopped, turning back. "Thank you Dart'aan. Thank you for helping me see what I was too stubborn to see before. " A grin tugged his mouth as he bowed low.

"A pleasure Mistress. Always a pleasure."

"You're still a manipulative bastard though," she called back over her shoulder. Dart'aan couldn't resist laughing out loud. Good, good. Things were back to normal between them. Now to see how she would handle San'zo. How indeed. He didn't really want to see the Earth Priest dead either. And he would be good for her. A quiet counterbalance to her harsh aggression.

"San? San, may I speak with you?" San'zo glanced up at hearing D'Challya's voice and immediately dropped his gaze.

"As you wish Mistress," he said softly. He thought back to Dart'aan's parting words, but he didn't believe that the monk was right. After all, why would the Shadow Priest care about him? What could he possibly be worth to her? He doubted that any would truly mourn his passing. No one except Lilin, his spirit helper. To her though, he was already dead. Thinking of the spunky dragon spirit made the despair and loneliness he was feeling only get worse. Why hadn't D'Challya let him die? This crushing despair was starting to weigh on his soul.

"San...I don't want to be a part of your death." He did look up at her now, a resigned expression on his face. So, he was going to have to kill himself—again. He wouldn't get the peaceful, painless death she had been able to offer.

"As, as you wish Mistress." He lowered his gaze once more, feeling tears slipping down his cheeks. D'Challya knelt down beside him. Reaching out she tipped his face up, forcing him to look at her. She noticed how beautiful his eyes truly were, frightened and sad though they were. San'zo's eyes were a rich azure blue color; the color of the Miriar Ocean in the summer. She reached up and brushed his tears away.

"San, I don't want to see you dead for any reason. It would wound me deeply to see you die, even more so if I had to be a part of it. I...I...," her own gaze dropped for a moment, "I find that I care for you Earth Priest. Grael help me, I care. If you're willing, let me be a reason to keep living."

She dropped her gaze again, speaking softer than he'd ever heard her speak, "And if not, then three days hence I will do as I promised. I will give you your final rest."

He was stunned. He hadn't expected the monk to be right. She did care, and it was the first time in a very long time that anyone had told him that. Or even hinted at it. San'zo had been orphaned at a young age, and with no bloodkin to take him in, he had been left to his own devices. Normally a village as a whole would take care of such an orphan, but his had done no such thing. For reasons he did not know, many had gone out of their way to make his life miserable. Finally, after enduring two long years of abuse, the young boy had made his way across Dunn'Mar to the Dragon Temple. The only people to know why such a young cub had come to the Temple in the first place were the Dragon Priests. He had told his story in full to Temple Master Sos'sno, who had related it to the others. He knew that Master Sos'sno had sent people to investigate, but he never found out what they knew. Nor had he cared to. Ul'jehera, then a Priest of Gaia, had taken San'zo under his wing. And when the elderly Earth Priest had passed away, it was San'zo who was chosen to take his place. That seemed like such a very long time ago. But even at the Temple he had found few friends. He kept to himself and the others let him do so.

He felt something loosen inside, and part of his overwhelming sadness diminished. He may still be cut off from Gaia, but now he had a reason to keep living. A reason to fight on. He felt some of his quiet confidence returning.

"I apologize Earth Priest. I should not have said anything," D'Challya murmured, interrupting his thoughts. She started to rise, keeping her gaze averted. San'zo stood as well, catching her sleeve.

"I'm willing—" She turned to face him and for once he met her gaze fully. "I'm willing if you are, Mistress." She smiled and relief washed the tension from his whippet thin frame. Standing, he towered over her.

D'Challya was not even five feet tall, whereas he was well over six feet, nearly as tall as a Trollen. She reached up and brushed his cheek with the back of her hand.

"Willing? Aye, I'm willing. I wouldn't have said anything if I wasn't. But," she paused and worry filled him again. But what? "But you're going to have to quit calling me Mistress." He heaved a sigh of relief.

"That I can do—Chal." He said the last tentatively, not sure how she would react. A ghost of a smile played on her lips and she opened her mouth to say something, but suddenly her eyes widened, filling with a nameless dread. She lost her balance and would have fallen if he hadn't caught her. He lowered her gently to the ground, panic filling him,

"D'Challya? Mistress, what's wrong?" She grabbed her head, shaking with rage.

"NO! No, no. No. Not again. Not another one. I'll kill them. Kill them all for this. Filthy humans." The words were spat out, in a snarling tone full of hatred. San'zo understood then. Another Priest gone.

"Who was it this time?" he asked quietly.

"Ar'jax," she growled. "Ar'jax is gone." Ar'jax, the Oracle of Bahamut. And it was far more likely that he was dead rather than captured. Ar'jax was a fighter, as M'Karr had been. Not an easy one to take as a battle captive. He hugged her close, seeking to calm her anger as she had calmed his fear before. She didn't try to pull away as he feared she might. Instead she buried her head against his shoulder, growling softly to herself. He rested his cheek against the top of her head, not realizing he was making the same soft, angry growls himself.

"Mistress! Mistress, it's not true is it? Oracle is no more?" Both Priests jerked up at the sound of Dart'aan's voice.

"How?" San'zo's voice faded as realization set in. D'Challya stood to face Dart'aan, bowing slightly.

"If you know that then I am your Mistress no longer. I welcome you among us Dart'aan, Oracle of Bahamut. A gain for a loss, no time wasted."

San'zo echoed her welcome. A slight stunned look on his face, Dart'aan replied with the formal words.

"I thank thee D'Challya, Claws of Grael. And thee as well, Earth Priest San'zo." Dart'aan bowed low to them in response. D'Challya reached into her robes and pulled out her jewel pouch.

"Choose wisely Oracle-to-be. Choose and we will raise thee to Dragon Priest by the will of the Patrons." He reached into the pouch and, not looking, pulled out a small blue stone. A star sapphire. "A wise choice Oracle-to-be, wise indeed." D'Challya's voice was changing, growing deeper and more menacing. Dart'aan looked up and gasped. The scarred eye was opened, her good eye shut. This eye was all ruby red, with no white at all. A vertical pupil ran the height of the eye. He dropped to his knees, noting that the Earth Priest was already kneeling.

"Lady Wardragon!" For the Shadow Priest was possessed by the Patron of Chaos herself. She laughed, a deep, malicious laugh, as she raised the jewel to his forehead.

"As Flame Priest Sos'sno and Freyeth aren't here to administer the rites, you are going to have to settle for me instead. A word of warning little Oracle—this is going to hurt. Are you prepared?"

"Yes, Mistress. I am prepared," his voice was barely above a whisper. She placed the cool jewel against his forehead, chanting the words of power to embed the jewel in his flesh and imbue it with the ability to channel dragon magic. Pain flared through his soul. An agony such as he'd never felt before. Then, it was over, and he could hear a stern, but comforting voice in his mind. Bahamut's voice. And another voice, a raspy one. Like the wind blowing through dry leaves in autumn. *My name is Calusari, Master. I am yours to call.* His spirit helper, Calusari. One of the lesser death dragons.

"Dart. Dart, stand up." D'Challya's voice was back to normal now. She continued to urge him to stand until he finally opened his eyes. Both Priests had gathered around, watching him anxiously. He gave them a weak grin and stood, rubbing a hand over his forehead as he did so. Sure enough, the star sapphire was there.

"I...I'm a Dragon Priest."

"Rreaallly. I hadn't noticed. Not only that, but you *would* pick the best jewel in my pouch." This from D'Challya, who was grinning at him.

"Congratulations Dart'aan. I'm sure you will make a fine...replacement for Ar'jax." San'zo's voice carried a wealth of sadness behind it. He was happy for the newly raised Priest, but this had only served as a reminder that he too would be replaced, eventually. D'Challya said that he hadn't

been so far, but it was only a matter of time. Dart'aan felt sorry for the Earth Priest. For himself, he still couldn't believe what had happened to him. One minute he had been happily practicing with his swords and he next he was being inducted into the ranks of the Priests. All this after braving the wrath of the Shadow Priest. What a crazy day.

Reunion

The three travelers were resting for the night, after a long day of walking. They had stumbled over the remnants of three Bear Clan villages over the past few days, but found no sign of any living Dunne'kaa. They had, however, found more humans than they would have liked, but had been unable to take a single one alive. Dart'aan had learned quickly how to use the dragon magic. But for all that he, like D'Challya, preferred to fight with weapons rather than magic. San'zo of course had no choice in the matter, but he had begun proving himself to be quite a capable fighter with the quarterstaff that was his chosen weapon. He was also considerably less depressed since the Shadow Priest had spoken with him. Dart'aan smiled over his half completed Sumatra, glancing up at the other two Priests. They sat close to one another, each absorbed in the tasks they were working on. D'Challya had taken it upon herself to carve his Patron emblem for him. All Priests wore the same gold robes, with the dark gold dragon on the back, and the Sumatra stoles and dragon jewels were unique to the individual, not the Patron. So, to let others know which Patron they were aligned with the Priests wore wooden emblems, representative of the Patrons, about their necks. D'Challya's was a black dragon claw, symbol of Grael. San'zo's was a beautiful red/gold leaf, one of the symbols associated with Gaia. So far it looked as if his was going to be a senshin, the Claw of Grael and the Healer's Flame of Ayahz merged as one. Together these separate symbols formed a whole, a blending of chaos and law. Much as Bahamut, being the son of Grael and Ayahz, was a blending of Chaos and Law.

San'zo worked on repairing the damage to his own Sumatra. He had decided to begin wearing it again, which Dart'aan thought was a good thing. That way he wouldn't forget that he was still a Dragon Priest.

As the light faded and night wore on, the three packed away their stuff, ate dinner, and settled down for sleep. D'Challya looked across the fire at Dart'aan. The Oracle looked tired and lost in thought. She was impressed at how quickly he had learned to use the basic dragon magic. He had even begun learning more complex magic. That was good. Very, very good. Now, if only they could capture a human alive to help San'zo. Then things would be perfect. Or as perfect as they could be when one's land was being invaded and one's people destroyed. It was now two days past San'zo's deadline and they still hadn't found a way to remove the collar. But he hadn't asked her to assist him after all. He did seem much happier now, after their talk. It was funny though. He would go out of his way to make her happy, to bring a smile to her usually frowning face, but often he acted fearful of being rejected. A part of him apparently couldn't believe that she really did care about him. He tried to hide these feelings of uncertainty, but more often than not he didn't succeed. D'Challya shook her head ruefully. She accepted him now as he was and would accept him as, Grael willing, he would be in the future, a Dragon Priest once more. She smiled as she remembered his shy, tentative question several days before, asking her to be his mate. Remembered the delight that had suffused his face when she'd said yes. The question, and her own answer, had taken her by surprise. The Dunne'kaa mated for life and never before had she even considered chaining herself to someone else for the remainder of her life. And the Dunne'kaa lived a very, very long time. The average Dunne'kaa lifespan was nearly 500 years and she was only 98. That was a very long time to spend with the same person. She found herself feeling grateful towards Dart'aan though, for forcing her to confront her own feelings. Left alone she probably would still be in denial. Or more likely she would have been plunged into her own depression, after fulfilling her promise to San'zo. Though most Dunne'kaa

knew their lifemates almost as soon as they met, she was still shocked at the whole turn of events.

Dart'aan was a brave monk to face down the Claws of Grael over anything. Throughout Temple history the most dangerous and temperamental Priests had been those belonging to the Lady Wardragon. And never before had a Dragon Priest taken a mate, much less the Claws of Grael! They were the ones least likely to ever take a mate. While not forbidden by the Patrons, it was just something accepted as not being done. All loyalty belonged to the Patrons. She wondered what her Patron thought about recent events. Grael must not be displeased. D'Challya sighed. She was tired and not really up to pondering whether or not she had made the right choice. It felt right and that was enough for her at the moment. Dart'aan had curled up for sleep while she had been musing over her thoughts and San'zo had already fallen asleep as well. She was the last one awake, exhausted, yet restless. She reached down and ran her fingers through the Earth Priest's hair, causing him to stir in his sleep. His hair was so soft. Dunne'kaa hair was soft in general, but his was softer than any she'd felt before. She curled up beside him and threw her cloak over the pair of them. Finally she drifted off to sleep, hearing the sounds of a quiet fall night.

The morning dawned, bright and cold. The Priests rose with the sun as usual, ate their breakfast, and began traveling again. They were still hoping to find more Temple monks, or better yet, another Dragon Priest. But no such luck. All they found were ruined villages, dead Dunne'kaa, and numerous human invaders. Five more days passed thus. Still, they kept fighting and kept searching. On the sixth day of their travels though, things changed and someone else found them.

Mistress. Yugi'shiro comes. The Windrunner comes. Azhi's deep voice made D'Challya look up in surprise. Judging from Dart'aan's expression he was getting a similar message from Calusari. Both Priests began scanning the skies, looking for the Wind Priest. Yugi'shiro, the Windrunner, was a Priest of the Wind Dragon Rai. And he was the only current Priest to have mastered any form of transformation. The Windrunner had the ability to transform into a half-dragon, with the wings, tail, and lower body of a dragon. It was this form that he preferred to stay in, as it was an asset in hand-to-hand combat. The claws on his feet were as deadly as any sword blade and the tail and wings could pack quite a punch if one were hit with them. Not only that, but his wings were fully functional, giving him the ability to fly. It didn't take Yugi'shiro long to find them, guided as he was by the spirit dragons. He landed with a thud that made the Patron emblem bounce against his chest, folding his wings about him like some kind of odd cloak. The Windrunner was a handsome male, though he was shorter than even D'Challya. He had long silvery hair that was pulled back, and eyes the color of a winter storm. A pair of ebony horns curled back from his head, giving him a rather fearsome appearance. He wore no gold robes, only the supter pants and shirt and his sumatra was wrapped about his throat like a scarf. His dragon feet and tail only added to his frightening appearance. Scaled in silvery gray the limbs were incredibly powerful and sported three huge claws each and the tail was strong enough to knock even the strongest person over.

"Greetings Shadow Priest, greetings Oracle. Congratulations and welcome." Yugi'shiro turned to greet San'zo and found himself at a loss for words. "Earth Priest San'zo! How—how is this possible?" the Wind Priest sputtered.

"It is a long story, Windrunner." San'zo pulled down his cloak to reveal the collar. "Apparently the humans have devised a way to shield us from the Patrons using these collars, which render our dragon magic useless. I am cut off from Gaia, cut off from Lilin. But I am still very much alive, in no small part due to D'Challya here." He offered the Shadow Priest a warm smile. Yugi'shiro looked from one Priest to another, confusion flitting across his face.

"I don't know what to say. I am sorry San'zo. Very sorry for your loss. I can't imagine what that must feel like."

"I thank you, Windrunner. My pain has grown less, but I have hope that we will find a way to remove the collar. And I have found other reasons to live." San'zo stepped back allowing D'Challya to take the lead.

"Windrunner, what news have you? Where are the others?"

"A large group of Temple monks along with several refugees turned fighters lie 3 miles west of here. Three more Priests would be a welcome addition. If you would be so kind as to follow me, I will show you the way."

They followed the Wind Priest, leaving the path and entering the forest. As they walked Yugi'shiro told them all that had been happening. He and his band had met much the same as D'Challya and hers. Humans everywhere, burned villages, countless Dunne'kaa out of homes or worse, dead. For all the humans they killed, twice that many took their place. The Windrunner had managed to find another group of monks and refugees though, with the Dragon Priests Yoshi'maru and Tani'mar leading them. Yugi'shiro was planning to bring his group to join theirs. It had been on the way back to his own group that Yugi'shiro had found D'Challya and the other two. By midday they had neared the Dunne'kaa camp. As they drew closer, the sounds of fighting reached their ears. More humans. The Dragon Priests raced forward, D'Challya and Yugi'shiro summoning their spirits as they went. By the time they reached the camp Azhi had joined them, as well as Quetzal, Yugi'shiro's spirit dragon. Quetzal had silvery scales, but where most dragons had leathery wings he had black-feathered wings. Feathers also ringed his neck making a crest around his head. Quetzal was one of the few dragons lacking forefeet. His wing-arms served this purpose when he was on the ground. The Wind Priest and the two dragons took to the sky. D'Challya, Dart'aan, and San'zo, meanwhile, had to settle for good, old-fashioned ground fighting.

The three charged into the overrun camp and immediately found themselves separated and surrounded. In the background D'Challya could hear Azhi and Quetzal and the screams of pain and terror that followed in their wake. She turned her attention to her own attackers.

"We're going to have some fun with you little dragon master." One big human twice her size edged towards her, a lewd grin on his face. The others snickered.

"Ya think? I seriously doubt you will be the ones having fun in this encounter," D'Challya snorted, feeling the blood hunger rising.

"This lets me think so little dragon master," the human held up one of the collars. Aah. Now that presented more of a problem. "You're surrounded, dragon master. You've no escape. We'll have you collared in no time."

"You'll find that more difficult than you imagine human. You've got to get close to me first." She watched the humans warily, chanting under her breath. As she did so a blue flame appeared in her hands. She grinned, "Care to dance human? Have you ever seen what dragonflame can do to a person? It burns so hot that it is impossible to put out. A body will be consumed by dragonflame in mere seconds. So....who wants to be first?" The humans backed off a bit, circling her cautiously. One lunged at her blind side and she spun to throw a fireball at him. The flame struck him full force in the chest. His screams died away quickly as the hungry dragonfire incinerated him, filling the air with the sickly sweet smell of burning flesh and hair. Two more tried their luck and met with the same fate. She snarled, baring her teeth. "So humans, who's next? This dance is a little more costly than you thought, now isn't it?"

"You can't stop us all at once little dragon master." At a gesture from the collar wielding human all of them rushed her at once. D'Challya had enough time to take two more out before she was dragged down and pinned to the ground, the fireball dissipating. She struggled fiercely, but try as she might she couldn't free herself. There were just too damn many pinning her down. The collar bearer loomed over her.

"Feisty are we? Just the way we like 'em." He grinned again as he leaned down to put the collar around her neck. Fear added strength to her struggles and she managed to get her legs up and give him a good, swift kick to the groin.

He dropped, wheezing in pain, as the others subdued her again. The big human managed to get to his feet and kick her hard in the side. "Oh, you're going to pay for that, Dunne'kaa. You are going to pay dearly." He reached down and pulled her head up by the hair, moving to put the collar around her neck.

"CHAL!" San'zo's cry startled the humans, so intent were they on getting the collar on her. The collar-wielder looked up just in time for his face to meet the end of the Dragon Priest's staff. The humans scattered before the angry Priest as he charged through them, staff whirling. His face was pulled back in a snarl and his normally warm blue eyes had turned as cold as ice chips. D'Challya stood and drew her kappen as the humans encircled the pair. Both Priests backed up until they were stopped by one another. D'Challya chanted under her breath again and shielded herself to prevent damage from weapons. Then she did the same for San'zo. Apparently the collars only prevented the wearer from using dragon magic. They did not prevent dragon magic from being used on the wearer.

"Manna fere, Chal. Much appreciated."

"I could safely say the same, San." No sooner had she completed the shields than the humans rushed them. Both Priests danced around each other, working in concert to bring their opponents down. The staff whistled through the air and the kappen blades flashed in the sunlight as the pair fought.

As they were finishing their battle D'Challya heard Dart'aan cry out in triumph across the camp. She turned to the sound of his voice and found him surrounded by humans in a myriad of odd positions, as if they had been frozen in the middle of fighting—which, in fact, they had been. The Oracle had gained the ability to use paralysis magic. She grinned. Good. Now they had captured humans to question about the collar, among other things. She surveyed the rest of the camp. Except for those frozen by Dart'aan, the humans were all either dead or had fled. Many of the Dunne'kaa refugees had fallen, as well as far too many of the Temple monks. D'Challya frowned and strode over to where Dart'aan stood, surrounded by the frozen humans, San'zo following behind her.

"Good work Dart'aan. Now maybe we can get some answers."

"Yes, very good work Oracle. Now, what are we going to do with them?" Yugi'shiro joined them and all three Priests turned to D'Challya. As the Claws of Grael, she was the senior most of all present. That meant she had to decide how to deal with them. Well, that didn't take much thought in her opinion.

D'Challya strode up to the nearest human. The prisoner was only able to move his head. His eyes were wide with fear and he was shaking. Hrrmph. Pathetic humans. They couldn't even face death honorably. And they had brought this on themselves after all.

"Human, I have but two questions for you. Answer them to my liking and you may survive this." He nodded, eyes growing rounder. "First, why are you here? Why have you invaded our lands with no cause?" The human shook his head, tears spilling down his cheeks.

"I don't know. The Emperor ordered us to attack the Dragon Lands. The Revered Father advised the Emperor that attacking the Dragon Lands and eradicating the Dragon worshipers would bring glory to the Empire and please the Gods. It was he who gave the Emperor the collars for binding the Dragon Priests and the enchanted metal to bring them down." He said the last in barely a whisper. She growled, causing him to flinch. Revered Father? Who the hell was this Revered Father who had given the Emperor's troops a way to defeat the Dragon Priests? She didn't realize that she had spoken aloud until she heard the human speaking again.

"I do not know his name, my lady. Nor does anyone know what he really looks like. He is always dressed in hooded robes. The Revered Father appeared in the royal court about five years ago and made himself indispensable to His Majesty." The Shadow Priest snorted.

"And that brings me to my last question, human. How do you remove the collars? I'm assuming there IS a way to remove them."

"Yes Mistress. There is a way to remove them. But I do not know what it is." D'Challya's face hardened.

"If that is true human, then I have no more use for you." In one swift movement she brought one of her kappen up and across his throat. The body tumbled to the ground, released from the binding spell. The Shadow Priest turned to the next human, who was shaking so badly he would have already collapsed if he weren't frozen in place. D'Challya heard someone approaching her blind side and glanced back to see one of the monks dragging a human female with him. Hmm. A human female. Out here? She was wearing tattered clothes and a brand of some sort was visible on her bare shoulder. D'Challya turned back to more pressing business, dismissing the female for the moment. One by one she questioned the males and one by one she coldly dispatched them when they couldn't provide the information she sought. The other Priests and monks didn't interfere with her. Many would have loved to exact a greater revenge on their captives, but they deferred to the Shadow Priest.

It was only after she finished executing Dart'aan's prisoners that D'Challya turned her attention to the human female. She had sunk to her knees, horror stricken by the ruthless efficiency with which D'Challya had executed the prisoners and she nearly passed out from fright when the Shadow Priest addressed her.

"Why are you here, human? The females of your kind rarely fight and you do not look like much of a fighter to me anyway." D'Challya's voice was a little softer and less menacing than when she was dealing with the males. But not by much.

"I belong...belonged...to the commander of the unit that attacked your camp. Please Mistress, please don't kill me. I never wanted to come here." D'Challya snorted again, causing the female to cower even more.

"You belong to the commander? You were his mate then?"

"No, Mistress. I was a slave. As I will be your slave now if you let me live." She was sobbing openly now, terrified of dying by the Dragon Priest's blades. A slave? She was a slave? What kind of a people enslaved their own? The Dunne'kaa didn't even take slaves from their enemies, much less among their own. They kept no captives of any kind. It was too much trouble and it was a practice frowned upon by the Patrons.

"I have no need of a slave, human. My people look down upon such a practice." The female began to sob even harder. She edged forward, moving close enough to the Shadow Priest to gather up the edge of the golden robes and kiss them. Fear made her voice hysterical.

"Please Mistress, please. I don't want to die. Please. The collars. I can help you with the collars you were asking about." That caught D'Challya's attention. She shook the human off her robes and knelt down in front of her.

"Indeed. Enlighten me human. And I would suggest that I find your information useful."

"Only the commanders know the secret of opening the collars." The female cringed at D'Challya's sharp look. "One learns things as a slave, Mistress. No one pays attention to us. And...much is said around slaves that would not be said around real people. I know how to open the collars."

"Well, human, we're going to put that to the test." D'Challya gestured and San'zo knelt down beside her, exposing the collar. "Remove this tasteless fashion accessory that your people have so kindly graced my mate with and you keep your life. If not...well I don't think I have to explain that now, do I?" D'Challya tapped one of the closed kappen against her cheek to emphasize her point. The human nodded weakly and reached out, placing her hand on San'zo's collar. She spoke then, singing words that made no sense to D'Challya's ears. As her singing ended the collar fell free, tumbling to the ground. San'zo looked down, dumbstruck, then reached up to feel about his neck. His face was glowing with joy, tears of happiness falling down his cheeks as contact was re-established. D'Challya watched him, an odd feeling growing in her. It was a warm feeling, one that calmed her nerves. It grew stronger, pushing against her mental shields and D'Challya realized that what she was feeling was San'zo. She dropped the shields and his consciousness flooded her mind. She was aware of the Earth Priest's thoughts, his feelings. Of his sheer joy. Of the depth of the love he felt for her. She could feel the link between him and Gaia, between him and Lilin. Not only that but she could tap into those links as well. Theoretically then, she should be able to draw power and magic from him. And he could do the same from her. Was it because they were mates that they had formed such a bond? A bond so similar to that between Priest and guardian?

The wind picked up suddenly, causing miniature dust devils to dance around. D'Challya could hear laughter in the wind. Delighted laughter. A tiny dragon appeared, one no larger than a wolf. It was very small for a dragon, yet the little one had the energy of one twice her size. Her scales glittered emerald in the sun. A black mane ran down her neck and she lacked wings. The Shadow Priest realized with a start that San'zo's dragon spirit was still a youngling. She hadn't yet matured into a full grown dragon. The tiny dragon bowled the Earth Priest over and twined around him like a cat. And like a cat, she purred, a deep rumble sound. D'Challya felt his happiness increase.

"Lilin! Lilin, I've missed you so much!" He wrapped the dragon in a bear hug. He turned towards her then, face growing serious for a moment. Confusion and awe tinged his features. "Chal...I feel you. In my soul itself. How is that possible?"

"I do not know San. I feel you too. I expect it has everything to do with the fact that we are both Dragon Priests," she smiled, "but I do not regret it in any way." He returned the smile and reached over the dragon in his lap to gently brush her cheek with his fingers. She caught his hand in hers and squeezed it before turning her attention back to her captive.

The female human had backed away from the Dragon Priests. She had pushed herself against the monk who had captured her, eyes wide with fear and focused completely on the dragon in San'zo's arms.

"Little human, you have done more for us than I ever could have hoped. You have won your life, if not your freedom. What is your name?"

"Zera," she replied, fear still evident in her voice.

"Very well, Zera. We will not harm you, but you will remain with us, as our guest. We will not bind you, but should you flee...the end results would not be pleasant. I trust you will not try to run from us."

"No, Dragon Mistress. I will not try to run."

"Zera, do not call any of us dragon masters. We are not masters of the dragons, we are their servants. Mistress or Master is fine when addressing any of the Priests, but not dragon master. Now, I will turn you over to So'Garin as he is the one who captured you." The Shadow Priest looked up at the monk. "So'Garin, you will take good care of our guest will you not?" So'Garin bowed low to the Shadow Priest and gathered Zera up.

"As you wish, Mistress." He bowed again and trundled off with his charge, leaving the Dragon Priests to decided the next course of action.

Transformation

The Dragon Priests had turned their group to the east and merged with Yoshi'maru's group. Now they were six Dragon Priests strong. Not only that, but they had nearly 300 Temple monks and twice as many fighter refugees. On the downside though, they had over a thousand refugees who couldn't fight. Women, children, elders. All of whom needed to be protected. But the best protection was in their large numbers. And with over half the Dragon Priests together *and* a way of unlocking the collars, should anymore be collared, they made for a very formidable force indeed. The biggest concern was the fact that the humans also had arrow points and crossbow bolts made of the same metal as the collars. It was this, presumably, that killed M'Karr and Ar'jax, and what had allowed San'zo

to be captured in the first place. Weapons that could penetrate the damage repelling shields of magic. Great. Something else to deal with. D'Challya sighed and surveyed the camp. What to do, what to do? She noted Dart'aan and Tani'mar were together, working on something and grinned. After the two groups had merged, a relationship had quickly grown between Dart'aan and Tani'mar, and between Yoshi'maru and Yugi'shiro. An unprecedented event. Not one, but three mated pairs of Priests. It seemed that the Patrons were urging their Priests to form relationships among themselves. But why? She frowned as she pondered this again. She had prayed to Grael, but received no answer to this question. Maybe it had something to do with the fact that the Dragon Priests gained the ability to share magic. Though it hadn't happened yet, D'Challya was sure that the magics could be combined, forming powerful new spells. It was only a matter of time.

"D'Challya?" Yugi'shiro's voice interrupted her train of thought and she turned to face the diminutive Wind Priest. "D'Challya, there is a large group of humans traveling towards the camp. They travel slowly and at the rate they are moving are still several days away, but if they keep to the path they are following they will run right through our camp here. There are also several smaller groups of humans but they are further behind the large one." Lovely. Just lovely. The dragon spirits had been sent out as scouts along with Yugi'shiro and all had reported to their Priests with an all clear. All of the humans they had spotted had been headed away from the camp. Several times Priests and fighters had gone out to engage the smaller groups, routing them with ease as none had any of the magic weapons with them. Yugi'shiro, however, was the first to report humans headed towards the camp itself. This wasn't good news at all.

"Yugi'shiro, let us call the Priests together. We must make our plans to deal with these humans. More likely than not we will end up fighting them."

"Yes, Shadow Priest. I will call the others together." Yugi'shiro bowed and smiled grimly. "Finally, a chance to do some real damage to the invaders."

"Do not be overconfident Wind Priest. They have already taken two of our number down with the enchanted weapons they have. We must plan carefully if we are not to add to the list." Yugi'shiro nodded and set off on his task, leaving the Shadow Priest to her musings. Yes, this may be a chance to deal a great blow to their enemies, but how many of their own would they lose? No doubt that such a large group would have enchanted collars and weapons. And Dunne'kaa prisoners. That was another thing Zera had been able to tell her. The humans were capturing Dunn'kaa when they could, to take back as slaves. Such thinking only made D'Challya grow angrier than she already was. Her sudden burst of fury brought concern from San'zo, filtering through the bond they shared.

Chal? Are you alright? She smiled as his voice filled her head. Yes, Dart'aan had been right. San'zo had been good for her, for he managed to help keep her temper in control during these trying times. Though it had not been more than three weeks since they had met, it felt as though they had been together all of their lives. She relaxed, letting go of her anger.

I am fine, San. As fine as I can be anyway. Yugi'shiro has brought distressing news. A group of humans headed this direction. He has gone now to gather the others that we might decide how to deal with this new problem.

And here he is now, with Dart'aan in tow. We will see you shortly in the Council tent. D'Challya sighed and started to make her way across the camp. The Council tent was in the center of the camp and big enough to hold all of the Dragon Priests if need be. She could only hope they found the others soon. There were four left out there, somewhere.

D'Challya and the others discussed their options long into the night, finally deciding that a direct assault that included four Dragon Priests and half of the total fighters available would be the best plan. Yugi'shiro and Yoshi'maru would remain at the Dunne'kaa camp to protect it, though they really didn't expect the camp to be bothered. Still, better safe than sorry. The rest would go to attack the humans. Finalizing their plans, they split up to get some sleep before the night was gone entirely, while runners were sent to alert all who would be going tomorrow. D'Challya and San'zo headed towards the tent they shared on the western end of the camp. Each pair of Dragon Priests had a tent located at separate areas of the camp, to allow for maximum protection should they be attacked. Dart'aan and Tani'mar stayed at the eastern edge and Yugi'shiro and Yoshi'maru stayed at the southern edge. Temple monks protected the northern area. This arrangement kept all of the refugees, fighters or not, inside a protective circle.

The sun rose on a cold, clear day. The Priests and fighters involved in the attack ate a quick meal and left before the morning had barely even begun. The group traveled swiftly and reached the humans later the next day. Before they ever got close they split up to ring the human camp. D'Challya stood with San'zo waiting for Azhi to confirm that the others were in place. She didn't have to wait long. *Mistress. All is ready. The humans are surrounded. We may begin.* The blood hunger welled in her mind, the battle lust that she shared with the demon dragon. She grinned, calling Azhi to her, granting him physical form. Nearby, San'zo likewise summoned Lilin. No doubt Dart'aan and Tani'mar were doing the same on the other side of the camp. So, four Dragon Priests, and four draconic guardians, now that Dart'aan had finished his sumatra. Calusari had truly been something to behold. The death dragon appeared in a skeletal form, with glowing blue eyes that shone like foxfire. The humans were sure to be even more terrified of him than any of the other spirit dragons. For some reason they feared the undead realm far more than the living, the spiritual, or the preternatural.

By now they had moved close enough to the camp that they could see and hear the humans. Before they had split up, the Dragon Priests had shielded all present from being seen, as well as shielded them from damage. All those so shielded could see one another, which went a long way in preventing them from running into one another. Barring being hit by the magic weapons, the warriors should be fairly safe. No regular weapons would hurt them unless the Dragon Priest who shielded them fell. She started to move forward, following San'zo. The Earth Priest stopped suddenly, motioning for her to do the same. She fell back, letting him feel her puzzlement. The feelings she received were pondering, as if he was considering some problem he wasn't too sure about. The spirit dragons stopped as well, focusing their attention on San'zo. The Earth Priest knelt down, chanting softly. As he finished the spell he plunged his fist into the earth. The ground rippled away from his hand like waves on water. The earth heaved and shifted, rising into great mounds. The mounds gained shape and form, becoming golems. Made of the earth itself these elementals would be very hard to defeat. San'zo looked up and grinned mischievously.

"New skill. Very useful I think." He turned to where the golems were patiently waiting for his orders. "Go now. Go and kill all the humans you find." The huge earthen behemoths moved off towards the camp and the Priests and dragons followed behind. They cleared the woods and entered the camp, screams of fear greeting them. Until the fighters or Priests struck a blow or received one they would remain hidden from view. This resulted in utter chaos among the humans as the Dunne'kaa appeared suddenly among them, felling several before the fight had even really started. Cries of terror followed in the wake of the dragon spirits, the loudest letting her know where Calusari must be.

She strode forward, drawing the kappen as she went. Chanting her own spell she set the gleaming blades ablaze with dragonfire. D'Challya chuckled. Anyone unlucky enough to be struck by these blades wouldn't live to tell of it, no matter where they were hit. She and San'zo charged into the fray, striking down a pair of humans before their cloaking shields were lost. Her victim screamed as he burst into flames, seemingly by himself. San'zo's victim blundered into hers in his fright and managed to set himself on fire as well. Stupid humans. Two down. Countless to go. She turned her attention to a group of humans in front of her. They backed away from her warily, eyes on the flaming kappen in her hands. Behind her she heard San'zo chanting again and then what sounded like the thump of his staff on the ground. The ground rumbled and geysers of earth shot into the air, pelting nearby humans with boulder sized chunks of debris. A few of the chunks managed to take out some of her opponents. Well now. That was one way to go about it. D'Challya lunged forward, dancing among the humans, seeking only to get one clean strike in. The flames did the rest of the job for her. Seeing so many of their comrades fall to her fiery blades many of the humans turned and fled, only to meet other Dunne'kaa. She chanted again, a longer, more complex version of the dragonfire spell and a ring of flame encircled her. She released it and the wave rushed out, incinerating any humans in its path. Those Dunne'kaa it washed over were protected by the damage repelling shields. She snorted and set off to find more humans to fight. This was too easy. Maybe way too easy. *Mistress! Go to the center tent! The largest one here. There are prisoners there. Some of the humans entered the tent and I fear their intentions are not good. Go now. Go. Go.* D'Challya ran, heeding the demon dragon's voice, making her way to the huge tent in the middle of the encampment.

Dart'aan had seen where D'Challya and San'zo had entered the camp. Those earthen monsters could only have been the Earth Priest's doing. Shortly thereafter he had been struck by D'Challya's flamewave. The firestorm had pushed against him, but not harmed him. It had, however, taken out all of his current opponents. That didn't seem to be a problem though as more surged forward to take the place of the fallen. He grinned and twirled the twin blades, teasing his enemies, taunting them to come to him. Already he had taken out more than his fair share of the humans. The Oracle laughed as he danced around, slashing here and there with the scimitars. Humans fell before him like grain before the reaper's blades. Dart'aan chanted under his breath while he fought and released a burst of the paralysis magic, freezing those humans around him. With a ruthlessness equal to the Shadow Priest's he cut them down and moved on, growling under his breath. The invaders would get no mercy from him. No more than they had shown to the countless dead Dunne'kaa they had left in their wake. Dunne'kaa who were not fighters in the least. A blast of crystalline shards struck Dart'aan. He frowned and glanced down. Ice fragments littered the ground. He looked over to where his mate, Tani'mar, was fighting. She was grinning like crazy and he suspected the shards had been her doing. After all, she was a Water Priest and of the two devoted to Tiamat, she was the better in offensive magic. He surveyed the camp and found that most of the humans were down. The bulk of the fighting was now concentrated towards the center of the camp. *Master, come quick. To the large tent in the middle. They have prisoners here, Master. I can smell them.* Dart'aan frowned. Dunne'kaa prisoners? Well now, that could present somewhat of a problem. He snarled in anger, turning to head for the tent and saw D'Challya running towards it as well.

The two Priests arrived in front of the tent at the same time. They pulled up short as a human, one of the commanders from the looks of his armor, came out. He was dragging a Dunne'kaa boy in front of him, a sword held to the child's throat.

"Back off dragon masters. Back off. Now." The pair edged back warily and the human moved forward, pulling the child with him. The boy's eyes were wide with fear and he called out to the Priests, pleading for help. "Quiet child. They can be of no help to you," the commander snarled, "Now dragon masters. I'd suggest that you call off the attack or this one will die. And so will all of the other prisoners." His captive started struggling madly, managing to break free somewhat and turned to latch onto his captor's hand with his teeth. The human howled in pain and flung the child to the ground. "Why you filthy little rat! How dare you. Leverage or no, you're dead." He brought the sword up and around, decapitating the child as he tried to flee to the dubious safety the Priests had to offer.

"Nnnnoooooooooo!" D'Challya roared. Her senses were surpassed by the blood hunger, rage flooding her. She fell to her knees, clutching her head. The world had gone so quiet. She couldn't hear anything at all, even though from the looks of it Dart'aan was talking to her, concern evident on his face. Her body felt like it was on fire, her blood itself was boiling. There was an odd sensation running through her body, making her feel as if she were coming apart. The world blacked out and she felt herself falling into oblivion.

Dart'aan jerked back to himself at the Shadow Priest's outraged cry. He couldn't believe it. The human had killed an innocent child. For no good reason at all. He glanced at D'Challya. She was kneeling on the ground, holding her head, evidently in pain. As he watched it looked as if something were moving under her skin.

"D'Challya? What is wrong? What is happening to you? " A brilliant flash of purple light engulfed her, causing him to shield his eyes. The light faded, with a reverberating roar louder than any he had ever heard before. Dart'aan looked up, and kept looking up. Where the Shadow Priest had been there was now an enormous black dragon. One eye glittered with a ruby malice from a head twice as large as Azhi's. Obsidian scales covered its body and great ram-like horns curled around horse-like ears. A mane of jet black hair ran down the creature's head and back. The Oracle was amazed. It had been a very long time since any Priest had the ability to completely turn into a dragon. He smiled grimly to himself, noting how much like Azhi she looked. Another deafening roar reverberated through the air and he turned to see yet another huge dragon, this one with scales the color of ripe wheat. The dun-colored dragon had a darker golden mane and spikes on the end of his tail. A pair of sapphire eyes glittered in the huge head. Now the Oracle was truly shocked, for the golden dragon could be none other than the Earth Priest. When one had gained the ability to transform, both had. It was then that Dart'aan noticed the glittering ruby and amethyst stones in the massive dragon heads. The dragon jewels had changed with them, becoming much larger versions of themselves. That was interesting. Above him D'Challya snarled and stamped her huge feet in agitation. He backed up, edging away from the angry black dragon.

D'Challya came to herself and was aware that something was wrong. For starters she was way high up in the air. She shook her head and noticed the human on the ground in front of her. He was looking up and looked like he wanted nothing more than to be elsewhere. From nearby came a dragon roar like none she'd ever heard before and she turned to see a great golden dragon. What the hell?! Where in the name of Grael had this dragon come from? He was huge, bigger than any of the dragon spirits.

Chal? Chal, we are dragons! We've managed to transform fully. San'zo's voice filled her head, and realization set in. The golden dragon was her mate. She looked down and found that she now had great clawed feet, scaled in glittering onyx. Well no wonder the human was terrified. He had every reason to be. San'zo roared again and she responded. The spirit dragons joined in and with them the Dunne'kaa cheered. She grinned wickedly, lips pulling back to reveal razor sharp teeth longer than sword blades.

"Well human, it seems I must thank you. After all, you pushed us into learning *this*. And now, it's time for you to earn your reward." Her head snaked forward and she caught the commander in her powerful jaws. She shook her head and flung the body away. Kill innocent children in front of her would they? She lunged forward and jerked the huge tent up, revealing the rest of the prisoners and several more humans in the process of trying to execute them. She snarled low in her throat and set about disposing of these humans as well, the prisoners flooding around her feet.

Within minutes the Dunne'kaa had cleaned out the human camp. They took no prisoners and tracked down and killed all the humans who had fled after D'Challya and San'zo had transformed. Dart'aan was shocked at the condition of the prisoners freed from the humans. They were nearly starved to death, with gaunt faces and baggy clothes where they had lost so much weight. And most were children. All of them had been beaten or worse, bearing fresh wounds and older scars from Bahamut only knew what kinds of torture. He smiled grimly. The Dunne'kaa had gotten their revenge though. They hadn't lost any Priests and very few fighters. The shields had held and the humans hadn't had any of their magical metal here to disrupt them. Hmm. That begged the question of where the humans with the collars and enchanted weapons were. Well, they would find them eventually. The next move for the Dunne'kaa group was to leave the ruined Bear Clan territory and head into Deer Clan. Ah, well that was for another time. For now, it was time to head back to the main camp.

***To read the complete first section of Dragon Jewels, please visit www.fictionpress.com and search for the author pen-name Sanzo-sochisama. Enjoy!

Dragon Guardians

By AnitaMK
I was called to meet up
Ascension was ahead
Among the others waiting
I was lined in front to embrace my fate

Other worlds where on hold
Calling us to go back home
To the place we once origin
Beyond galaxies; beyond everything we already know

The dragons are watching over
So that non will walk out from the neutral line
Those that try escaping
Will be doomed at once with no regrets in mind
Flames from dragon will burn

Through those untrue to the Divine source
Those that believe they are the answer
To forever salvation through destruction of truth and time

Dragon slayers will come on by
Ready to hit and wrong the sacred guardians
But those true dragon friends and fighters
Will face them without any doubt in mind
Now the time has come for those already chosen
Those that are lined in front
To be tested truthfully
Judging from their soul, heart and mind

Dragon Guardians they will become
A duty to embrace and hold
As those that have guardian dragon,
Will be guarding the dragon in return

Peace there will be when we all remember
That the source of all life is one and the same
Once this is accepted and acknowledge
That's the day dragon and human; will live united as one and the same

Crystal Dreams
By EsselDel

High on the slopes of the Mystical Mountains is a place where unicorns and dragons live. In the sides of the bright, stony mountains are caves made out of magickal glowing rock, and in one of these caves lives a sparkling purple and green dragon called Narlith.

Narlith is a very small dragon with a very important job. In his cave are great mounds of rainbow, sparkling crystals, and Narlith spends his days filling these crystals with good dreams and loving thoughts. In the evenings

he takes the crystals he worked on that day and flies on the cool breeze toward the Flowering Meadow, where, at the exact moment that dusk turns into night, the Planet Portal opens. It is through the swirling white portal that Narlith travels to all the worlds that are losing their magick. Narlith takes the crystals to those worlds so that hope can live again!

Narlith's job is a special job and the little dragon is happy to do it. He was pleased to hear the unicorns and dragons talk of how the crystals helped the worlds and made their jobs so much easier. However, good as Narlith's work was, what he'd always wanted to do was venture to the other planets the way that the other people of the Mystical Mountains did. He wanted to meet the people living on the planets and do something for them in his own special way. So one evening after another day of playing with the baby unicorns who collected the crystals for him and filling the crystals with their happy games, he decided he would stay behind on the planet that he visited that night to see what happened with his work. And maybe then he could meet with the people who found the crystals.

Narlith flew over the graceful mountains and arrived at the Flowering Meadow just as the portal burst open. He flew into the white tunnel, and it let him out on the other side over a small planet with pale blue forests and bright pink seas. Narlith, carrying his sack of crystals in his claws, glided down to the planet surface and after flying around for a while, found a clearing surrounded by blue and purple trees. It was close to a small town, so he placed the crystals in the middle of the clearing where he thought the people might find them. Then he flew up into one of the trees to perch and wait for people to come by in the morning.

In what seemed like no time at all, Narlith awoke. He'd fallen asleep, but woke in time to see the glittering stars in the night sky turn into dawn as the red sun poked over the hills in the distance. Just as it did, Narlith thought he heard laughter and watched with delight as a boy and a girl, both with silver skin and golden hair, walked through the trees and into the clearing. They were getting ready to have a race to see who could pick the most berries from the bushes at the edges of the clearing when they spotted the pile of crystals.

"Look!" said the boy. "Magick crystals!"

"They weren't there yesterday," the girl said excitedly as she ran over to them. "Somebody must have put them there in the night. Oh! What if it was a dragon?" She sounded delighted by her idea of a dragon.

The boy shook his head as he reached the crystals. "Jenny, you know the grown ups say there's no such thing as dragons." He told her.

"Uncle Bernie says they're real, remember," she reminded him. "And you know how I've been wishing and wishing that a dragon would come so that everybody would know that magick really does exist!"

Narlith ruffled his wings and swished his tail happily as he sat in the tree. Now he knew exactly how he could help: by being himself!

"Well, if there is a dragon, it will come to us right now." The boy said loudly so that if there was a dragon in the trees, which he expected there wasn't, it could hear him. Narlith certainly did hear him, flying from the branch and landing right in front of the children so they could see him. They both gasped in surprise and the girl cried, "It came true! My wish came true!"

Their race forgotten, the children picked the berries for breakfast as quickly as they could, gathered the crystals at Narlith's suggestion, and urged him to come back to the town with them. Narlith agreed happily and he walked back through the lush forest with the excited children.

When the people of the town first saw Narlith, they were shocked, for none of them had ever seen a dragon before and most of them thought that none existed. The children explained what had happened and Narlith told them that he would not hurt them, and very soon the people were fulled with joy. They had celebration and singing to welcome Narlith, and were so happy to know that magick had not forgotten them. Narlith told them stories about unicorns and the Mystical Mountains and how his crystals would bring them good dreams and good luck. Uncle Bernie, who looked after the children, was especially pleased to see him and told him, a little shyly, of a dragon he once met. Narlith knew the dragon too; it was Carmen, a big white dragon. Uncle Bernie was so delighted to find that a dragon really had visited him and he wasn't just dreaming it after all!

All too soon the day was coming to an end and the people tried to coax their excited children to go to bed. Narlith was also thinking about going home, but he'd enjoyed the day with the town's people so much that he didn't want to leave. But he knew he'd have to leave soon because he had to tend his crystals. How could he go home and keep helping these people at the same time?

Just as Narlith wondered as much, a pure white glowing creature walked out of the forest and came toward the town. As it got closer the people could make out its form, a shimmering white steed with a single, golden horn.

"It's a unicorn!" Somebody cried in awe and the people of the town welcomed her as eagerly as they'd welcomed Narlith earlier. She was Narlith's friend Einsal, and though she was very happy to meet everyone, she explained that she and Narlith would not be able to stay.

"The worlds need your crystals, Narlith," she said. "The people of Mystical Mountains want you to come home. But there's no need to worry about these people here, because we unicorns have a surprise for you that means you will know whenever they need you." She turned to the towns folk. "If you ever need Narlith, then all you have to do is call for him."

The unicorn would tell no more about the surprise, so Narlith bid his new friends farewell and promised to return. Einsal used her magickal horn to open the Planet Portal in the sky, and they were back in the Flowering Meadow.

When they got back to his cave, Narlith found a group of glowing unicorns waiting for him with pleased smiles on their faces. They pointed to the floor by his pile of crystals with their horns and moved aside to let him see. There, made out of polished stone and surrounded by the nicest of his rainbow crystals, was a shimmering pool of water. When he looked into its depths he could see an image...the silver people as they slept peacefully in their town.

"Now you can watch over the people you meet on your travels *and* keep making Crystal Dreams," Einsal told him. The other unicorns agreed with whickers and nods. Narlith gave a delighted flap of his wings that made the waters of the watching pool ripple. Now he had everything he'd ever wanted!

Chapter 4

Dragons in the Natural World

Long ago, when man was young and the dragon already old, the wisest of our race took pity on man and gathered together all the dragons making them vow to watch over man always. And at the moment of his death, the night became alive with those stars. And thus was born the dragons' heaven.

—Draco, from *DragonHeart*

Dragons in the Sky

Dragons have always been important to man. We have even found them in the stars themselves. There are three main dragon constellations in the night sky.

Draco: The constellation of the dragon is the eighth largest constellation in the sky. Draco winds around the sky close the North Pole, and in most northern latitudes never sets. Thuban is Draco's brightest star. More than 4,000 years ago Thuban was the North Star. Today, the north star is Polaris, located at the tip of the handle of the Little Dipper. Thuban is the third star from the end of the dragon's tail. Draco's head is a boxy group of stars positioned north of the bright star, Vega; its long body winds towards Cepheus, then turns and runs west between the Big and Little Dippers.

Hydra: The constellation of the sea serpent is the largest and longest constellation in the sky. At mid-northern latitudes it takes more than six hours for the whole constellation to rise. It is sometimes called the female water snake, because in Latin the name is feminine. Its head is south of Cancer and east of Canis Minor. Its body snakes east almost as far as Scorpius.

Hydrus: The male water snake is a small constellation close to the South Pole. It is a modern constellation named by Johann Bayer, published in his 1603 atlas to fill in an area near the south celestial pole. There are no mythological associations with this constellation as there are with Draco and Hydra. Hydrus is bordered on the west by Tucana and on the east by Mensa and Dorado.

Dragons in the Ancient World

Dragons have dwelled in the minds of men for as long as we can remember. As we have seen, one theory behind dragons is that they were based on real creatures. So, what kinds of creatures could have inspired giant, lizard-like creatures? Well, dinosaurs for one. People never saw the real creatures that the bones of dinosaurs belonged to, but they had to belong to something. So why not dragons? There are a great many dinosaurs and other extinct creatures that could fit almost every category of dragon.

Sea Serpents and Dragon Whales

Basilosaurus: This proto-whale's name means "Regal Lizard." Despite being called an early or primitive whale, these creatures were not the ancestors of our modern whales. They belonged to an ancient group called archaeocetes. Basilosauri averaged 50 feet long, but some specimens have been recorded at 80 feet in length. These creatures had elongated vertebrae all along their backbones; relatively short necks; and narrow, tapered heads. Basilosaurus could flex its body side to side, like a serpent. Its main mode of navigation, however, was by undulating up and down. Sound familiar? This type of movement was exclusive to sea serpents. Basilosaurus had flippers for forelimbs that were jointed like a seal's elbow joint, giving it greater maneuverability. Basilosauri had vestigal hind-flippers, but they were not of much use. Basilosauri lived during the Eocene epoch.

Zygorhiza: This member of the archaeocetes is the more likely candidate for being the ancestor of our modern whales, both toothed and toothless. Zygorhiza had elongated bodies like their cousin basilosaurus, but they were not quite as large. They did, however, share the feature of short necks and long, tapered snouts. Zygorhiza had prominent and versatile fore-flippers and vestigial hind-limbs with the evidence of knees and toes still present. Zygorhiza, like the basilosaurus, lived during the Eocene epoch.

Mosasaurus: These were ocean-dwelling marine reptiles that resemble today's snake more than lizards. Mosasauri dominated the shallow seas of the late Cretaceous period. Mosasauri were crocodilian in appearance, but had longer forelimbs with elongated finger-paddles and atrophied hind-limbs. These creatures were far more stream-lined for fast underwater swimming than modern crocodilians. Mosasaurus had a loosely-hinged jaw full of sharp teeth. This special feature allowed them to swallow food whole, much like snakes can. In length mosasaurus averaged about 40 feet. Some mosasaur sub-species were as small as 6 feet in length, while others grew to as large as 60 feet in length.

Plesiosaurs: These marine saurians typically had broad bodies, short tails and four well-developed flippers. It is believed that the plesiosaurs evolved from the older nothosaurs. There are several different families of plesiosaurs, including the plesiosaurids, elasmosaurids, pliosaurids, and cryptoclididae.

Elasmosaurus: This long-necked member of the plesiosaur family lived during the Cretaceous Period. Its name means thin-plated lizard due to the thin bony plates in its pelvic girdle. Elasmosaurus averaged about 40 feet in length, most of which was neck. These creatures had big, bulky bodies, extra long necks, small heads, and four paddle-like flippers.

Plesiosaurus: This marine reptile lived during the Jurassic period. It lends its name to the order of Plesiosauridae, being that it was the first of this order discovered and named. The name itself means "near lizard." Similar to many other members of the Plesiosauridae, plesiosaurus had stout bodies with four fully developed flippers, longer than average necks, and a tapered head full of sharp teeth.

Placodonts: This group of flat-toothed marine reptiles lived in shallow oceans rather than the deep sea. They ranged from 6-10 feet in length. Most placodonts superficially resembled the walrus and dugong of today, but many had armored, turtle-like plates along their backs. All had stout, robust bodies and short limbs with heavy claws.

Ichthysaurs: These fish lizard marine reptiles of the Triassic looked similar to fish, just as the name implies, but with reptilian snouts and flippers. They had huge eye sockets set in a stubby head with a long, tapered snout. The smallest were some 70 centimeters in length, while the largest exceeded 40 feet.

Drakes

Ankylosaurs: These armored dinos are relatives of the stegosaurs. Quadrupedal plant-eaters, ankylosaurs were low to the ground. All sported bony plated armor and spiked or clubbed tails. As with the stegosaurs and the ceratopsians, ankylosaurs had parrot-like beaks with specialized teeth.

Ankylosaurus: This fused lizard ranged in length from 25-35 feet. It is perhaps the best known of the ankylosaur family. Its entire back, neck, and head were covered with thick oval plates set into its leathery skin. A row of spikes ran along each side of the body, just below the ending of the armored plating. A ring of larger spikes adorned its neck and it had a blunt, clubbed tail. This dino was among the longest of its family, yet the last to evolve. Ankylosauri lived during the Cretaceous period.

Euoplocephalus: Another creature of the Late Cretaceous period, this dino with the well-armored head grew to lengths of roughly 20 feet.

Euoplocephali had toothless beaks. In appearance, they much resembled the contemporary ankyylosauri, but also sported great horns on the sides of the head.

Panoplosaurus: This totally-armored lizard of Late Cretaceous in North America reached lengths of up to 23 feet. Panoplosauri had armored plating along their backs, necks, and heads. Small spikes protected the head and a row of spikes ran along each side from the front of the body to the middle. Plating covered the hindquarters and the spikes picked up again behind the rear legs and extended down the tail.

Ceratopsians: The ceratopsian, or horny-faced dinosaurs are very good candidates for drakes. These dinos were quadrupedal with beak-like snouts and frills/horns around their heads and faces. The ceratopsians were the biggest dino family, with species ranging from the size of a pig to nearly twice the size of a rhino.

Chasmosaurus: This frill-face reached lengths varying from 18-25 feet. Chasmosauri, or "chasm lizards," sported two small brow horns, one small nose horn, and a broad, bony neck crest tipped with many small spikes. As with many ceratopsians, Chasmosaurus made its home in North America during the Cretaceous period. Interestingly, fossilized examples of Chasmosaurus skin have been found. This skin has a knobbly, pebbled texture to it.

Styrachosaurus: This frilled dino lived in Late Cretaceous in North America. Its name means "spiked frill" and it sported a six-spiked frill around its neck. Styrachosauri also sported one large nose spike and two smaller brow spikes. Similar to all of the ceratopsians, Styrachosauri were four-footed plant-eaters with parrot-like beaks. These beasts reached lengths of 18 feet.

Triceratops: This well-known three-horned face ceratopsian had two very large, prominent brow horns and a smaller nose horn. A great bony crest ringed the neck. Triceratops could reach a length of 30 feet, with 10 feet being the head alone! Like Styrachosaurus, Triceratops lived during the Late Cretaceous period.

Hadrosaurs: These duck-billed dinos could reach lengths of 30 feet and heights of up to 15 feet. They walked both quadrupedally and bipedally. All sported duck-like snouts and most had fancy crests or other head adornments. These crests were hollow, allowing the dinos to create unique sounds through them. Preserved hadrosaur eggs and skin fragments have been found.

Hadrosaurus: These relatively plain duckbills were the first of the family discovered, thus giving the beast its name. They had no crests at all. Hadrosauri reached lengths of 23 feet and heights of 10 feet and lived during the Late Cretaceous Period.

Maiasaurus: This "good mother lizard" sported only a small bump in front of the eyes. It lacked the crests and elaborate headpieces that other duckbills are known for. Maiasauri grew to lengths of 30 feet long and lived during the Late Cretaceous period. Maiasaurus was the first dinosaur to be found alongside nests of young and eggs, earning it the name of "good mother lizard" to begin with. It was a fragment of Maiasaurus eggshell and leg bone that flew with astronaut Loren Acton during the eight day long Spacelab 2 mission.

Parasaurolophus: The better known of the elaborate duckbills, Parasaurolophus had a long, backturned, hollow bony crest that was the length of the entire head! Parasauolophi grew to be 40 feet long and 8 feet high. Like the other duckbills, Parasaurolophus lived during the Late Cretaceous period.

Megalania prisca: This ancient lizard roamed the Australian wilderness during the last great Ice Age. Megalania was stockier and shorter than its later cousins, but still a much larger beast. These great drakes could reach lengths of up to 30 feet and weighed in at half a ton, making it the largest lizard to roam the world.

Pachycephalosaurs: These thick-headed dinos are cousin to the frill-necked ceratopsians. They were bipedal with thickened skulls full of bony protuberances. Their dome shaped skulls could grow up to 8 inches in thickness.

Pachycephalosaurus: This thick-headed lizard sported a 10-inch-thick, dome-shaped skull ringed by bony spikes all the way around. It is believed that these dinos used their heavy heads not for butting heads, but for butting other animal's flanks. Thick skulled or not, it would not have been in the dinos greater interests to go around butting heads. Pachycephalasauri grew to heights of 15 feet. Like so many other dragon candidates we've studied thus far, these giant plant-eaters dwelled during the Late Cretaceous Period.

Stegoceras: This "roof-horned" dino only grew to about 7 feet in height, making it a small member of the pachycephalasaur family. Like its bigger brothers, Stegoceras had a thick skill (about 3–4 inches) which was ringed with small spikes, though not nearly as many as the Pachycephalasaurus.

Stygimoloch: This "demon from the River Styx" dwelled during the Late Cretaceous modern day Wyoming. Like other Pachycephalasaurs, Stygimoloch had a dome-shaped, thickened skull ringed with spikes. This dino grew to 7–10 feet in height.

Sauropods: These gentle plant-eating giants are truly drakes if any dino ever was. The name sauropod means "lizard footed." If the T. Rex and its ilk were the biggest carnivores to roam the earth, Brachiosaurus and its brethren were the largest herbivores to roam it. All sauropods were quadrupedal and had extremely long necks.

Apatosaurus: Better known as the brontosaurus, or the thunder lizard, this dino's true name means "deceptive lizard." Apatosauri grew to lengths of 70–90 feet and heights of 17 feet at the top of the fully raised head (10 feet at the shoulder). Its head was small—a mere 2 feet of the entire body length. Most of the length was given over to a long neck, a huge body, and a long whip-like tail. An apatosaurus neck alone had 15 vertebrae! These dinos lived during the Jurassic period North America.

Brachiosaurus: One of the tallest and largest dinosaurs ever found, this creature gets its name "arm lizard" from the fact that its front legs, and not the back ones, are the longest. Brachiosauri reached 85 feet in length and a whopping 50 feet tall with the head fully elevated. Brachiosaurus lived during the Jurassic period.

Diplodocus: This "double-beamed lizard" is among the longest animal to ever walk the planet. It was some 90 feet long, with 26 of that being devoted entirely to the neck and 45 to the tail! The tail was whip-like and likely used as a first line of defense. Recently found skin impressions show that the diplodocus had a row of short spines running down its back.

Stegosaurs: These four-footed plant-eaters had small heads and stocky bodies sporting plates along the spine. Many also sported spikes on the tail tip. The plates, once viewed as a defense, are now believed to have served some sort of solar energy function by helping to absorb heat.

Kentrosaurus: This spiked lizard of the late Jurassic period had small, armored plates from its neck to its midsection. From the midsection back it sported a double row of long, sharp spikes that ended at the tail-tip. Kentrosauri grew to lengths of some 17 feet. Like its brethren, Kentrosaurus had a small head and its brain was only the size of a large walnut!

Stegosaurus: This "roofed lizard" was some 30 feet long and 8 feet tall. It had two rows of alternating plates running from the neck to the end of the tail. The very tip of the tail was adorned with four wicked, long spikes. These dinos lived in Late Jurassic period in modern day North America.

Wyverns

Pterosaurs: These flying lizards usually sport long bird-like snouts full of teeth, leathery bat-like wings, and a long tail. Some had fur on their bodies and some sported bony head-crests that may have served a rudder-like function. Pterosaurs, like modern birds, had only two sets of limbs—

the forelimbs which turned into wings, and hind-feet. There is some controversy as to whether ground-bound pterosaurs walked on all fours as a bat might or on two feet, with the wings folded, as a bird does. These creatures ranged in size from a few inches in length to upwards of 40 feet in length.

Pterodactylus: One of the smaller pterosaurs, this little guy had a wingspan of only 30 inches. It sported a small head crest and had no tail. Pterodactylus lived during the Late Jurassic period, usually along lakeshores.

Pterodaustro: This South American pterosaur dwelled during the Late Cretaceous period. It had long teeth designed to strain food, much like the modern flamingos. It is believed that the pterodaustro's diet may have given it a pink hue similar to the flamingo as well. Of course, this is mere speculation and conjecture! Similar to pterodactylus, pterodaustros had a relatively small wingspan of some 52 inches.

Pterodon: This pterosaur of the Late Cretaceous period was about 6 feet in length with a 25 foot wingspan. Pterodon sported an elongated and very prominent head crest and lacked a tail.

Quetzalcoatlus: Named after the mythical dragon Quetzalcoatl, this pterosaur was the largest animal to ever fly our skies. This giant beastie had a whopping wingspan of some 40 feet, and yet weighed an estimated 110 pounds! Quetzalcoatli had small, knobby head crests and lacked a tail.

Early birds: Early birds likely evolved from the raptor species, which we will cover in the dragons section that follows. The first feathers were modified scales and more recent conceptual art has given such creatures as the velociraptor and troodon primitive feathers. Most early birds still had long bird-like beaks full of sharp teeth, wing claws, and a bony tail.

Archaeopteryx: This "ancient wing" bird hailed from the Jurassic period and is often credited with being the first bird. Only about the size of a modern crow, archaeopteryx had a bill full of conical teeth, three claws on each wing, hollow bones, a bony but feathered tail, and a wishbone.

Though it had feathered wings and could fly, this ancestor of our modern birds could not fly fast nor very far.

Ichthyornis: This early "fish bird" lived along the shores during the Late Cretaceous period. Ichthyornis is believed to be one of the first early bird species to sport the keeled breastbones that help modern birds in flight. These birds had toothy beaks and big heads. They were also rather small, being only some 10 inches in length.

Mononykus: This single clawed bird was a small insect-eater of the Late Cretaceous period. It had relatively short arm-wings with a single long claw each, long thin legs, and a long tail. Mononyki were small, being only about 28 inches in length.

Sinornis: This early Chinese bird of the Late Cretaceous period was roughly the size of a sparrow. It had a more bird-like beak full of small, sharp teeth, three small wingclaws to each wing, and feet perfect for gripping branches. Sinornis is believed to have been an excellent flier but a rather poor walker.

Dragons

Ceratosaurs: These were bipedal meat-eating dinosaurs that sported four-fingered hands, arching, lightweight skulls, and horns on the snout or head. However, these horns were more decorative than dangerous.

Ceratosaurus: This horn lizard of the Late Cretaceous period sported a small horn on its nose. In addition, it had smaller eye ridge horns and bony horns on the top of its head. These fearsome creatures were powerfully built predators some 20 feet long. It is believed that ceratosauri hunted in packs, thus allowing them to take down much larger sauropods as well as compete with the larger carnosaurs.

Coleophysis: This small hunter is one of the oldest ceratosaurs and believed to be one of the oldest predacious dinosaurs. At a mere 9 feet long, coleophysis, or "hollow formed" dinos, had light, hollow bones. Unlike many other ceratosaurs, these had just three claws per hand, as opposed to four per hand. They also had snouts full of sharp, serrated teeth. Coleophysis lived in Triassic South Africa and North America. Similar to their later cousins, it is believed that they, too, hunted in packs.

Dilophosaurus: This double-crested lizard is probably best known from the hit movie *Jurassic Park.* While it is not known if dilophosauri had crests like frilled lizards, they did sport double head crests. These small, slender hunters lived during the Late Jurassic Period. Dilophosauri were 20 feet long and 5 feet tall.

Carnosaurs: As the plant-eating dinos grew in size, so did the meat-eating dinos. Among the largest of these great predators were the carnosaurs. These beasts weighed in at several tons and exceeded lengths of 50 feet. A skin impression found of a carnosaur showed it to have fine scales accented with larger scales. Most carnosaurs had heavy bodies and shortened forelimbs.

Allosaurus: Probably the best-known of the carnosaurs, Allosaurus was the largest meat-eater to walk in the Late Jurassic period in modern day North America. This lizard gets its name from the fact that it had vertebrae differing from other dinosaurs. Allosauri were some 40 feet long and 16 feet tall, with the skull alone exceeding 3 feet in length. This terrible hunter had small brow horns and bony ridges above the eyes.

Baryonyx: This unusual heavy-clawed carnosaur of the Late Cretaceous sported longer than average forelimbs and a longer, more crocodilian snout. Its most unusual feature, though, were the heavy, foot-long claws on its hands. Another striking feature was the straight, short neck, as opposed to the S-shaped design favored by so many other predacious dinos. Baryonyx attained lengths of some 32 feet.

Carnosaurus: A "flesh-eating bull" of the Late Cretaceous period, Carnotaurus gets its name from the pair of bull-like horns that jutted from its skull. This dinosaur sported smaller forelimbs than even the later tyrannosaurs would. Carnotauri reached lengths of 25 feet.

Megalosaurus: This great lizard of the Jurassic period was the first dinosaur fossil to be discovered in Britain. Megalosauri were some 30 feet long and 10 feet tall. They sported small bony bumps on their heads, especially near the eye ridges. As with most of their brethren, megalosauri had heavy bones, bulky bodies, and large snouts full of sharp teeth.

Raptors: These small, fleet predators are best known for the giant machete-like sickle claws on each foot. These were among the smartest of dinosaurs and the ones our modern day birds are believed to have evolved from. Indeed, the name "raptor" or "thief" is given over to our modern birds of prey. Raptors sported rigid tails for balance, slenderer snouts, longer arms and bigger eyes than their larger tyrannosaur and carnosaur cousins. It is believed that these dinosaurs may have hunted in packs.

Dromeosaurus: This swift lizard is a founding member of the raptor clans. These small raptors had larger jaws and smaller claws than their later relatives.

Megaraptor: This huge thief of the Late Cretaceous Period was a giant among the raptors. At 26 feet long, megaraptors fit right in with the smaller carnosaurs like Carnotaurus.

Troodon: This raptor, whose name means "wounding tooth," was roughly the size of the average human. That is, some 5–6 feet tall. Troodon are believed to have been the smartest dinosaurs to walk the earth. In some circles of speculation, Troodon are the top picks for who would have evolved to modern human intelligence if the dinosaurs hadn't met an untimely end. These swift hunters lived during the Late Cretaceous Period.

Utahraptor: This "robber from Utah" was another of the giant raptors, topping out at some 23 feet in length. They lived during the Late Cretaceous period. I'll give you just one guess as to where!

Velociraptor: These swift hunters were made popular by the movie *Jurassic Park,* though true Velociraptors were not nearly as tall. In fact, they only reached about 3 feet tall and some 6 feet long. It is believed that these denizens of the Late Cretaceous period may have reached speeds of 40 miles per hour.

Tyrannosaurs: These magnificent tyrant lizards deserve the title of dragon if any ever did. Topping the predacious dino charts at over 50 feet in length, the tyrannosaurs sported the longest teeth of all the dino species. All had stocky bodies, heavy bones, short forelimbs, and huge heads attached to muscular necks. It is believed that these giant hunters could have attained ages of some 100 years before passing on.

Albertosaurus: This lizard from Alberta lived during the Late Cretaceous period in modern day Canada. Though smaller than its royal brother, the Tyrannosaurus Rex, it was no less fearsome. Albertosauri were about 30 feet long and 13 feet tall.

Carcharodontosaurus: This shark-toothed lizard lived during the Late Cretaceous period in modern day North Africa. Though larger than T. Rex, Carcharodontosauri had smaller brains. Amazing for a creature whose head alone was some 6 feet long! These dinosaurs reached lengths of some 40–45 feet.

Nanotyrannus: This "dwarf tyrant" of Montana was the smallest of the great tyrannosaurs, only reaching 17 feet in length and 7 feet in height. Originally the fossils were thought to be from an Albertosaurus and later that of a juvenile Tyrannosaurus Rex. Nanotyrannus was officially classified as a species unto itself after a CAT scanned revealed differences in its skull composition.

Tyrannosaurus Rex: The great "tyrant lizard king" is perhaps one of the best known dinosaurs of all. *T. Rex* lived in the Late Cretaceous period in modern day North American and Mongolia. Once believed to be the largest predator (only to be ousted by its slightly larger brethren Carcharodontosaurus and Gigantosaurus) this king among lizards was some 40 feet long and 20 feet tall. A T. Rex skull has been measured at a whopping 5 feet long, whilst their arms were a mere 3 feet long.

Dragons in the Modern World

Let it not be said that the dragon is forgotten in the modern world. There are a great many modern day animals that could be called dragons. Imagine coming upon a giant Nile crocodile, having never seen one before. Or worse, coming face to face with a Komodo dragon, the largest monitor lizard alive today. It is entirely possible that contact with vicious, predatory eels of sea and salt water gave rise to sea serpents.

Lizards

American Alligator: The name "alligator" comes from the Spanish phrase "el lagarto" meaning "the lizard." American alligators inhabit the southeastern United States, including such areas as the Carolinas, Florida, Texas, and Oklahoma. Male alligators typically reach lengths of 14 feet, but there have been the rare reports of giant 20-foot-long specimens. Females reach lengths of about 10 feet. Alligators have broad jaws in which the teeth of the lower jaw fit into neat depressions on the upper jaw, enabling the snout to close fully. There is a slight bony nasal ridge along the snout. Adult alligators are an olive black/brown color with a creamy colored belly. American alligators are among the largest and most vocal of the reptile species existing today. If threatened or disturbed, they will rumble and roar, sounding like an angry lion!

Bearded Dragon: These stocky Australian lizards have prominent spines along their sides and broad triangular heads. These little dragons sport spiny jaw pouches around the snout. When filled, the pouch looks like a spiky beard, designed to make aggressors think twice before attacking. There are many types of bearded dragons, varying from grays to bright oranges, browns to sandy khakis. When angered, bearded dragons flatten their bodies, fill the spiny pouches, and stand erect on their hind-feet mouths gaping open. These little lizards only reach about 1 1/2 to 2 feet in length and have become popular pets.

Chinese Alligator: Mostly restricted to the Anhui Province of China, these alligators are also known as Tou Lung or Yow Lung. Sound familiar? Remember, "lung" is the Chinese word for dragon, so the Chinese clearly do view these large reptiles as cousins of the dragon, if not the dragon itself. Chinese alligators are small, reaching only about 7 feet in length, though there have been reports of giant 10 foot alligators. These alligators have bony plates along the upper eyelids, unlike their American cousins. They also have slightly upturned snouts. They are quite adept at crushing prey with their massive jaws.

Flying Dragon: These tiny lizards get their name from being able to glide from tree to tree with glider wings that are located between the sets of limbs. These are formed from large patches of skin stretched along the length of extended, movable ribs. Usually these flaps are flattened against the lizard's sides, but when extended, can allow it to glide for a distance of several meters. Flying lizards are only some 7–8 inches in length and dwell in areas of the Philippines, Malaysia, and Indonesia.

Frilled Lizard: Also called frilled dragons and bicycle lizards, these reptiles are about 8-9 inches in length. They live in Australia (along with bearded dragons). Frilled dragons get their name from a frilled crest that usually remains at rest along their shoulders. This crest is opened when the lizard is frightened or needs to be intimidating, making it seem much larger than it really is. It also rears up on its hind-limbs and gapes its mouth open. If frightened, it will run away using only its hind-limbs, earning its second nickname of bicycle lizard.

Gila Monster: This venomous lizard of the southwestern United States and Mexico grows to be about 2 feet in length. It is the only known venomous lizard in the United States. Gila Monsters have thick, short tails and broad, blunt snouts. They are reddish-pink and black, with the snout being completely black. Gila Monsters can survive for months without food, living off the fat stored in their tail.

Iguana: Iguanas run the gamut in habitats and in color. There are desert varieties, marine versions, and those that live in rainforests. Perhaps the best known types of iguanas are the blue and green varieties, both of which are kept as pets. These lizards can grow up to 5 feet in length, though most of this is made up by a whip-like tail that is used as a weapon when the iguana is angry. Iguana have blunt snouts, a dewlap under the chin, and a series of spines running down the back, from neck to just behind the back legs.

Komodo Dragon: This is the world's largest known lizard living today. They grow up to 8–10 feet in length and weigh about 300 pounds. Komodo dragons are fierce hunters which have been clocked at some 11 miles per hour, which is relatively fast. They have large jaws, stubby legs, and sharp claws. As with many lizards, the tail is much longer with respect to the rest of the body. These lizards dwell on the Indonesian islands, specifically on the island of Komodo.

Nile Crocodile: The crocodile gets its name from the Greek krokodeilos, meaning "pebbled worm." Unlike their cousin alligators, crocodiles have long, narrow muzzles. The Nile crocodile lives in Egypt, along the Nile River, as well as in many other places in Africa. They average about 15–18 feet in length, though there have been rare reports of some nearly 24 feet long.

Snakes

Anaconda: This serpent is the largest snake in the world. It also goes by the name of water boa, and spends most of its time quietly waiting in shallow water for unsuspecting victims to wander by. These giant serpents live in South America. Anacondas continue to grow for the rest of their lives, reaching reported lengths of some 38 feet. Anacondas are greenish-brown with a double row of spots on the back and smaller, white markings along the sides.

Boa constrictor: These South American serpents do not attain the size of their anaconda cousins, yet they are impressive nonetheless. They reach lengths of 13 feet, though there have been reports of 18 foot long ones in the wild. Boas come in many colors, from gray to brownish red. All have spots or blotches of a darker shade over the length of the body. Boas are often kept as pets.

Python: These beautiful African serpents are related to the boas and anacondas of South America. They can reach lengths of some 15–20 feet and come in a great many colors and varieties. Like the boas, these modern wurms are often kept as pets.

Eels

Anguilla: There are many different types of Anguilla, with varieties common to America, Australia, and Europe. These sea serpent creatures can grow to lengths of more than 7 feet. They are aggressive creatures, with mouths full of barbed teeth. Anguillas have serpentine bodies with a mane-like fin running along the top and bottom of the body from the mid-section to the tail tip. These eels can travel onto land in search of food, using their strong fins to pull them along. They range from green to brown to black in color.

Conger: As with the Anguilla, there are several varieties with the largest growing up to 10 feet in length and weighing some 250 pounds. These serpentine creatures are very aggressive. Like their cousin anguillas, congers have mane-like fins running from the midsection of the body to the tail-tip. They, too, have mouths full of barbed teeth and can spend extended periods out of the water.

Moray: There are many different types of moray eels found all across the globe. The largest of these reaches some 12 feet long! Morays like to hide in holes in reefs. They are shy animals, but one you would not want to tangle with. They have mouths full of sharp, barbed teeth which they aren't afraid to use. As with most other eels, morays have a mane-like fin running from just behind the head and around the midsection to the tail-tip. These wonderful sea serpents come in many colors, including spotted and striped varieties.

Bibliography

Allen, Judy and Jeanne Griffiths. *Book of the Dragon.* London, UK: Orbis Books, 1979.

Allen, Tony and Charles Phillips. *Land of the Dragon: Chinese Myth.* New York: TimeLife Books, 1999.

Alten, Steve. *The Loch.* Portland, OR: Tsunami Books, 2005.

Arakawa, Hiromu. *Fullmetal Alchemist.* Lincoln, NE: Funimation, 2005.

Ashman, Malcolm. *Fabulous Beasts.* Woodstock, NY: Overlook Press, 1997.

Baldwin, Neil. *Legends of the Plumed Serpent.* New York: Public Affairs, 1998.

Borges, Jorge. *Book of Imaginary Beings.* Avon, OH: Avon Books, 1969.

Breath of Fire IV. Playstation game. Capcom, 2000.

Burland, Cottie. *Feathered Serpent and Smoking Mirror.* London, UK: Orbis, 1979.

Burton, Maurice. *Encyclopedia of Reptiles, Amphibians and other Cold-Blooded Animals.* Dublin, Ireland: Octopus Books, Ltd., 1975.

Carter, Frederick. *Dragon of the Alchemists.* E. Matthews, New York : 1923.

The Cave. DVD. Directed by Bruce Hunt. Sony Pictures, 2005.

Clair, Colin. *Unnatural History.* London: Abeland-Shuman Limited, 1967.

Cohen, Daniel. *Encyclopedia of Monsters.* New York: Dodd, Mead and Co., 1982.

Collins, Andy, Skip Williams and James Wyatt. *Draconomicon.* Wizards of the Coast, Inc., New York: Nov. 2003.

Cooper, J.C. *Symbolic and Mythological Animals.* New York: Aquarian Press, 1992.

Courlander, Harold. *Treasury of African Folklore.* New York: Crown Publishers, Inc., 1975.

Curran, Bob. *Creatures of Celtic Myth.* London: Sterling Publishing Co, Inc, 2000.

Davis, F. Hadland. *Myths and Legends of Japan.* New York: General Publishing Co., Ltd., 1992.

Dickson, Gordon. *The Dragon and the George.* Delray, Fl: Delray, 1986.

Dickson, Peter. *Flight of Dragons.* New York: Harper and Row, 1979.

Dragonheart: Collectors Edition. DVD. Directed by Rob Cohen. Universal Pictures, 1996.

Dragonheart: A New Beginning. DVD. Directed by Doug Lefler. MCA Home Video, 2000.

Dragonslayer. DVD. Directed by Matthew Robbins. Paramount Pictures/ Walt Disney Pictures, 1981.

Dungeons and Dragons: Wrath of the Dragongod. DVD. Directed by Gerry Lively. Warner Home Video, 2006.

Eggleton, Bob. *Book of the Sea Serpent.* Woodstock, NY: Overlook Press, 1998.

Ellis, Richard. *Monsters of the Sea.* New York: Alfred A. Knopf, Inc., 1994.

Final Fantasy VII. PSX game. Squaresoft, 1997.

Final Fantasy IX. PSX game. Squaresoft, 2000.

Final Fantasy X. PSX game. Squaresoft, 2001.

Fire Emblem: Path of Radiance. Gamecube. Nintendo of America, 2005.

Fire Emblem: Path of Radiance. Gameboy Advance. Nintendo of America, 2005.

Frazer, James George. *Golden Bough: A Study in Magick and Religion (3rd edition).* New York: Macmillan, 1915.

Gifford, Douglas. and John Sibbick. *Warriors, Gods and Spirits from Cen tral and South American Mythology.* London, UK: Wallingford, 1983.

Gould, Charles. *Mythical Monsters.* London, UK: Allen and Co., 1886.

Harry Potter and the Chamber of Secrets. DVD. Directed by Chris Columbus. Warner Bros., 2002.

Harry Potter and the Goblet of Fire. DVD. Directed by Mike Newell. Warner Bros., 2005.

Harry Potter and the Sorcerer's Stone. DVD. Directed by Chris Columbus. Warner Bros., 2001.

Heuvalmans, Bernard. *In the Wake of the Sea-Serpent.* New York: Hill and Wang, 1986.

Heuvalmans, Bernard. *On the Track of Unknown Animals.* New York: Rupert Hart-Davis, 1958.

Huxley, Francis. *The Dragon: Nature of Spirit and Spirit of Nature.* London, UK: Thames and Hudson, 1979.

Ingersoll, Ernst. *Dragons and Dragonlore.* Concord, NH: Payson and Clark, 1928.

Johnsgard, Paul. and Karen. *Dragons and Unicorns: A Natural History.* New York: St. Martin's Press, 1982.

Jones, David. *An Instinct for Dragons.* New York: Routledge, 2002.

Kellogg, Marjorie. *Dragon Quartet.* New York: Daw Books, 2006.

Lehner, Ernst. *A Fantastic Beastiary.* New York: Tudor Publishing, 1969.

Lessem, Don. & Glut, D. *The Dinosaur Society's Dinosaur Encyclopedia.* New York: Random House, 1993.

The Lord of the Rings Trilogy. DVD. Directed by Peter Jackson. New Line Cinemas, 2001-2004.

Lowery, Shirley Park. *Familiar Mysteries: The Truth in Myth.* London, Oxford University Press, 1982.

Lunar: Silver Star Story Complete. PSX. Working Designs, 1999.

Lynn, Elizabeth. *Dragon's Treasure.* New York: Ace, 2004.

Lynn, Elizabeth. *Dragon's Winter.* New York: Ace, 1999.

Mackenzie, Donald. *Myths of China and Japan.* New York: Gramercy Books, 1994.

McCaffrey, Anne. The Dragonrider Pern Trilogy. Delray, Fl: Del Ray Publishers, 1986.

McGowan, Christopher. *Dinosaurs, Spitfires and Sea Serpents.* Cambridge, Mass.: Harvard University Press, 1983.

Mode, Heinz. *Fabulous Beasts and Demons.* London: Phaidon, 1973.

Mulan. DVD. Directed by Tony Bancroft and Barry Cook. Walt Disney, 1998.

The Neverending Story. DVD. Directed by Wolfgang Peterson. Warner Bros., 1984.

Newman, Paul. *Hill of the Dragon.* New York: Bowman and Littlefield, 1980.

Nigg, Joe. *Wonder Beasts: Tales of the Phoenix, the Unicorn, the Griffen and the Dragon.* Wesport, Conn.: Libraries Unlimited, 1995.

Passes, David. *Dragons: Truth, Myth and Legend.* San Francisco, Calif: Western Publishing, 1993.

Poignant, Roslyn. *Oceanic Mythology.* Washington, D.C.: Paul Manlyn, 1967.

Priess, Byron., Betancourt, J. & DeCandido, K. *The Ultimate Dragon.* Rock Round, TX: Dell, 1995.

Reign of Fire. DVD. Directed by Rob Bowman. Touchstone Films, 2002.

Rose, Carol. *Giants, Monsters and Dragons.* New York: Norton Paperback, 2001.

Salvatore, R.A. *Dark Elf Trilogy.* Renton, Wash.: Wizards of the Coast Inc., 2000.

Salvatore, R.A. *Icewind Dale Trilogy.* Renton, Wash.: Wizards of the Coast, Inc., 2002.

Spirited Away. DVD. Directed by Hayao Miyazaki. Studio Ghibli and Buena Vista International, 2001.

South, Malcolm. (edt.) *Mythical and Fabulous Creatures.* Westport, Conn: Greenwood Press, Inc. 1987.

Stevenson, Jay. *The Idiot's Guide to Dinosaurs.* Phoenix, AZ: Alpha Books, 1998.

Tolkien, J.R.R. *The Hobbit.* Boston, Mass.: Houghton-Mifflin, 1999(reprint).

Troop, Alan. *The Dragon DelaSangra.* Lisle, IL: Roc, 2002.

Troop. Alan. *Dragonmoon.* Lisle, IL: Roc, 2003.

Weis, Margaret. and Tracy Hickman. *Dragons of Autumn Twilight.* Renton, WA: Wizards of the Coast, 2002(reissue).

Weis, Margaret and Tracy Hickman. *Dragons of Spring Dawning.* Renton, WA: Wizards of the   Coast, 2002(reissue).

Weis, Margaret and Tracy Hickman. *Dragons of Winter Night.* Renton, WA: Wizards of the   Coast, 2002(reissue).

Weis, Margaret. *Mistress of Dragons.* Evanston, IL: Tor Fantasy, 2004.

Whitelock, R. *Here Be Dragons.* Sydney, Australia: George Allen and Unwin, 1983.

White, T. H. *Book of Beasts.* London, UK: Jonothan Cape, 1954.

Zallinger, Peter. *Dinosaurs and Other Archosaurs.* New York: Random House, 1986.

Index

About the Author

Ash "LeopardDancer" DeKirk, B.A.(Grey)
Dean, Department Alchemy & Magickal Sciences
Dean, Department of Divination
Professor of Beast Mastery
Instructor in Alchemy & Magickal Sciences, Ceremonial Magick,
Dark Arts, Divination, Lifeways, Lore, and Magickal Practice
Lodgemistress, Order of the Dancing Flames

Professor LeopardDancer is a university graduate specializing in dragons and dragonlore. She holds a B.A. in anthropology and is hoping to go for a Masters in history or English at some point in the future.

Her hobbies and pasttimes include reading (all the time!), writing, and games of all sorts. She is in the process of writing a fantasy novel, as well as a modern translation of the Chinese folk-legend *Journey to the West*.

Ash DeKirk is a Graelan priest of the Dun'marra. She lives in North Carolina with two roommates Heather and Mike and their giant pet family: Rufus, Drizzt, Bakura, Tseng, and Tia (kitties), Artemis (rat), Roy (gerbil), Cinnamon and Sirius (birds), and her own personal pet dragon, Nobunaga (the python).